The Unmasked Villain

Chris Witt

Copyright © 2024 by Chris Witt

All rights reserved.

No part of this book may be reproduced in any form or by any electronic or mechanical means, including information storage and retrieval systems, without written permission from the author, except for the use of brief quotations in a book review.

❦ Created with Vellum

Introduction

In the dark alleys of a small town lies a ghastly secret, desperate to be uncovered.
When a series of heinous crimes plague their town, Detective Sarah Miller and Professor Zachary Barnes form an unlikely alliance to put a stop to it all.
During their investigation, they are forced to team up with an incarcerated criminal who reveals something bone-chilling, setting off a spiral of unexpected events.
It's a test of their nerves to the core.
Sarah and Zachary soon find themselves stuck in a rabbit hole of puzzling clues and eye-opening revelations—everything keeps getting more and more convoluted! While time is running out, a concealed piece of evidence may just bring them closer to the moment of truth.
Could the enemy be someone they know?
Just when Sarah and Zachary think everything is settled, they are thrown a challenge nothing could have prepared them for.
The tension is mounting, and the stakes are higher than ever.

Prepare for suspense that grips you and reels you in with riveting thrills and revelations! *Unmasked Villain* will keep you guessing until the very end. Are you ready to plunge into the darkness with Sarah and Zachary?

Chapter 1

The Dark Secret

The cloth I'd fit around my chest made it hard to breathe and buttoning up my borrowed uniform's overcoat only made it worse. It was obvious that the bit of tailoring I had done hadn't been enough. As uncomfortable as I was, though, I knew I needed to act as if nothing was wrong. The first two days working at the station had been easy; everyone wanted to let poor, almost-drowned Thomas take things slow after months of recovery. That generosity was gone now, though. Most of the officers had already been busy with the mass amounts of missing person reports that had been coming in, leaving me as one of the few who could investigate when the corpse was reported.

Seeing a dead body for the first time wasn't as bad as I feared. She'd been laid down in the middle of the alleyway with her arms folded over her stomach. The array of garbage had been moved out from under her, the cobblestone creating a nest of rotten food, discarded linen, and waste around her.

Her dress, though completely soaked from the rain,

looked clean and well cared for. The basques she wore extended her waistline and featured a dark green ribbon around the neck while the skirt of her dress was made of a thin, pink cotton. Her black hair had been put into a simple braid and decorated with a few white pearls. A glance at her feet showed them to be bare.

Looking over her, there wasn't a single visible injury or mark. She didn't even look dead; the low light of the lantern was strong enough to show how rosy her cheeks were. If I pushed everything else aside, I could tell myself that she was just sleeping.

"Do we know who she is?" I asked, making sure my voice was gruff.

Officer Conner shook his head. "Not yet. When we get back, I'm going to cross-reference it with the missing person reports."

I watched as he stepped up to the body and started moving her around. Something about the image of such a young man, someone barely older than my nephew, manhandling a body like it was nothing made me sick.

"I'm going to pop over to the other end of the alley. See if there's anything we missed," I told him.

He hummed in response, not even bothering to take his eyes off the woman as he turned her onto her side. While a part of me wanted to sigh and chew him out for his rudeness, I bit my tongue. It was probably only because of Conner being relatively new at the station *and* being so closed off that I'd been able to get away with my charade for the past few days.

I turned and carefully made my way through the trash. While it wasn't a part of the less-than-reputable area of the city, it did border it. While faint hints of light from the streetlamps a few blocks over managed to break through, the area was mostly dark. It would have been all too easy for someone to hide their actions in such a place.

"No wonder no one noticed them."

I looked over my shoulder toward the woman. Conner's lamp made it easier to see her now, but in the dark, it must have been nearly impossible to see. I thought back to what I'd been told about the report from the man who discovered the body. He stated that he was attempting to walk home from getting drinks at the pub when he tripped and landed right next to the body.

"Conner! Would you turn off the lamp?"

"Yes, sir."

With the lights gone, it was impossible to see anything. I started to make my way through the alley. Even without being drunk, each step was a struggle. It didn't take long for me to lose my footing and come crashing down onto the ground face first. While the garbage cushioned my fall slightly, it quickly crumbled under my weight and I felt myself being shifted with it. A stabbing pain along my chest stood out against the dull aches from my knees, nose, and forehead. When I sat up, the chest pain grew worse. I brought my hand up to the spot and winced when I found that it was wet.

Conner turned back on the lamp and, while it was hard to see against the dark fabric of the coat, the red seeping through my pale fingers were clear.

In a moment, Conner was kneeling down next to me with a clean handkerchief.

"Take off your clothes. We need to stop the bleeding."

"What? No—" I moved my one hand to tighten around the top of the coat while the other kept pressure on the cut —"it's fine. I'll take care of it on my own later."

"Don't be ridiculous. Besides your own safety, we need to preserve the crime scene."

"No! I can handle it myself—"

"Stop moving around and let me—"

The two of us continued to struggle for a while. The more reluctant I was, the more persistent Conner became. After a while, it was painfully clear that I was hiding something. From the way that Conner's brow was furrowed, I knew that the only way I was going to get out of this was if I attacked him.

As I was trying to figure out some other option, he managed to force the overcoat open. The dress shirt, the undershirt, and the binder would have been enough in most cases, but the blood and rain had soaked the fabric and had it pressing against my skin. Conner slowly moved his hands away from me and I knew that he had figured me out.

"Get up." Though he'd been distant and cold before, his voice was harsh now. "We're going to the constable."

* * *

The interrogation room that they'd left me in was cold but the officers had done what they could to make it more comfortable. I'd been given a small blanket when I was first brought in and it hadn't taken long for someone's wife to come by with a spare dress for me. I'd switched into the slightly large dress and began tending to the gash along my chest. When I finished changing, Officer Conner came in and took away Thomas's uniform.

An hour later, Constable Eric Fear came in. His uniform was perfectly pressed and he would have looked put together if not for the way that his graying hair had started to stick up at the top. He'd clearly been running his hands through his hair again. When he took the seat on the other end of the table, it was easy to see how tense his entire body was.

I put on a smile and took the initiative. "Hello, Eric. It's been too long. How's the grandbaby? I heard you and your wife had to take him in?"

"He's doing wonderfully, thank you." He gave me a smile but it was too stiff to be genuine. "How's Thomas?"

"The same as he was six months ago, I'm afraid. Though, you'd know that if you visited." I did my best to fight off a small smile when the constable winced at my words.

"I'm sorry about that. I've wanted to but..." He shook his head. "Why were you impersonating your brother?"

I sat up straighter. "We both know that being an officer means the world to Thomas. When he gets better, he'll want to get right back to work."

"And?"

"And I know that the world didn't stop turning just because one man is... *sick*." I swallowed hard, but the tightness in my throat was still there. "I saw that you're hiring. You're looking to fill his role. And, well, I figured that wouldn't be necessary if he were here. And, since the two of us are twins, I figured, what's the harm? If there's anything Thomas can do, I can do it too."

"Sarah, you can't—"

"Can't what? It's not illegal to dress like an officer. And I never said I *was* Thomas. Your officers just assumed as much for some reason."

"Right. Of course. And, you decided to cut your hair identical to your bother's because...?"

I felt myself blush. A part of me still missed the brown

5

curls, but there was nothing that could be done to bring them back. "Women's fashion is ever-changing."

Constable Fear shook his head. "If it's a money issue—"

"I'd have gone back into making clothes," I bit back, trusting that he didn't know enough about the time and effort required to make even a basic shirt. Even if I was worried about money, it really was only a part of it. "I'm trying to do right by my brother."

"But if it *was* a money issue, I'm sure that there are many officers here, myself included, who would be more than happy to assist you until you could find a more suitable position for yourself. And I'm sure John or James would be willing to help the two of you out."

I gripped the fabric of the dress and let out a small, shaky breath. John had been struggling enough with handling everything that had happened since he'd seen Thomas, his father, half-dead in the hospital. And, even though he wasn't related to us by blood, James was finding it just as hard to watch as the man who was more of a father to him than his own could barely move. Not to mention they both had to worry about rent and working up enough funds to get into college.

There was no way I could let them know I was struggling. "Am I being arrested, Constable?"

"No."

"Then, may I leave?"

"I suppose."

"Excellent." I stood up from the table and pulled the blanket closer around myself. "Then, I will. Please let the officer who lent me this know that I'll return his wife's clothes as soon as possible."

With my head held high, I walked out of the room and made my way toward the front of the building. Everyone I passed glanced at me, but I refused to acknowledge any of them. I was almost out of the building when Officer Conner stepped in front of me.

"I've been told that I should apologize for my behavior."

"No need, officer." I spoke around clenched teeth. The eyes of everyone in the station were directed right at us and I wanted nothing more than to hide away at home. "Just focus on finding the killer."

Conner laughed. "Already done."

"Pardon?"

"There were no signs of any injuries or struggle. The woman most likely laid down and died of natural causes."

"No, she didn't."

"Ms. Miller—"

"No." The blanket fell down to the ground but that didn't stop my entire body from feeling hot. I could barely stop myself from shaking as I continued on. "She wouldn't have just laid down. She wasn't even wearing any shoes! And you can't say that it was because she wasn't well off: she had pearls in her hair! On the off chance she decided to keep those rather than protect her feet while she walked around London, why would she have gone to such a filthy place?

"And that doesn't even begin to touch on her dress! She was wearing a basque that didn't match with her pearls *or* the skirt of her dress! The lower half wasn't even full! Why would she have half-dressed herself?

"Then, there's the inconsistencies with the report! Why do you think I asked you to turn off the lantern? Did you think I *wanted* to scamper around in the dark? No! It was to see what the man who reported the body saw—which was nothing! Clearly—"

I slammed my mouth shut when I heard a deep chuckle

from behind me. Whirling around, I found myself face to face with a man in a tweed suit. His dirty blond hair and mustache had been perfectly groomed and it was only the slight wrinkles around his brown eyes that hinted he was older.

"That's a keen eye, Miss." The man looked over me, toward Conner. "You may wish to take the lady's words to heart. Now, would you mind pointing me toward the constable? I have some business to attend to."

"Of course, sir." Conner's voice was tight as he talked. "Right this way."

I watched as the pair walked back down the path I had come from. While some of the officers watched them with curious eyes, others kept them pointed at me. I felt myself flush. Reaching down to grab the blanket, I wrapped it around me as a shawl and hurried out of the station.

Chapter 2

Plagued Community

The lights in the house weren't lit when I arrived home. Grabbing the candle from the side table, I made my way up the stairs toward Thomas's door. I knocked and waited. When he finally hummed a few minutes later, I walked in.

Very little had changed from when I'd left in the morning. The curtains were still open and the clothes I'd placed on the chair next to the bed had been left untouched. The plate that I'd brought breakfast up had been moved from the side table and was now on the edge of the bed. Most of the food had been eaten, but a bit of bread and jam was still there. The cup on the nightstand was half-empty and at least a third of it had clearly landed on the bed and Thomas, who, at the very least, had managed to sit up at some point.

For a moment, I just stared. I could almost see the ghost of my brother in the hunched form looking at the bookcase across from him. The brother I knew would never have let himself get so disheveled though. Even when we were kids, he'd be a neat freak; his hair would always have to be the right length and his clothes always had to be perfect.

I shook my head to focus on the sight in front of me.

"Were you hoping to read something?" I walked over to the shelf and began looking through the titles. Most of the works were Dickens's. I took the most worn one and made my way to the chair. Moving the clothes to the ground, I sat down and forced a smile. "How about *Nickleby?*"

He slowly turned his head toward me and grunted. Opening the novel to the first page, I began to read aloud. It was still a little difficult to some of the words, but Thomas didn't seem to care when I stumbled over or gave up on some of the harder to understand parts.

We'd only managed to make it partway through the opening of the novel when a knock ran through the house.

"J'hn?"

I smiled. "Probably. I'll go get him."

I handed the book to Thomas before walking out of the room. As soon as I'd closed the bedroom door, I started to hurry from room to room to light the lamps and straighten things up a little. By the time I made it to the door, the knocking was getting more insistent.

With a deep breath, I dusted off my dress—a dress that I could only hope John didn't comment on not actually belonging to me—and opened the door.

"Ah, good evening. Ms. Miller, correct?" The man in the tweed suit from the police station smiled at me before giving a slight bow. "I don't believe I properly introduced myself earlier today. My name is Zachery Barnes. I'm a professor of medicine at King's College. May I come in?"

"Of course, Professor. It's an honor. Is there anything I can get for you? Tea? Biscuits? A, uh..." I began circling my hand in the air, trying desperately to remember what we actually had in the house and not just "King's College"—"Milk?"

The Unmasked Villain

"No, no. That's quite alright. May I just..." He nodded his head toward the door and I felt myself blush.

Stepping out of the way, I let Barnes inside. "Right. Yes. Of course. Forgive me. I just wasn't expecting anyone."

I quickly led the professor past the stairs and into the drawing room. The space was small and the furniture, a round wooden table between two cream-colored love seats, was clearly aged. Even the wallpaper, a white with black floral designs, looked dusty. The only saving grace was that, since no one had used the space in ages, there wasn't any clutter.

I took a seat and gestured toward the other sofa. "I assume this is about the boys?"

"Sorry?"

My stomach dropped. "John, my nephew, and James Bullard? They're looking to study at your institute?"

"Ah, I see. Well, I look forward to meeting them. I'm sure they're quite brilliant. But, in truth, I'm here to speak with you. You mentioned that there were some inconsistencies with some report while at the station?"

"I did. The man who reported the crime had clearly lied. He couldn't have tripped on the body as he claimed or else the garbage would have been flattened." I looked down at my hands which still had a number of small cuts on them. "As I proved."

"He could have been exaggerating?"

"Then how did he see the body? He didn't have a lamp. And the moment Officer Conner turned off ours, it was impossible to see anything."

Barnes leaned forward. "So, you believe that he..."

"How am I to know? I didn't get to talk with him afterward."

The response made Professor Barnes smile. "Excellent.

Jumping to conclusions is what leads to misdiagnoses. Ms. Miller, how would you like to be my assistant?"

"Pardon?"

"My assistant. The constable has approved my request to observe some of the deceased in cases to better understand how we might help people. And the woman you and Officer Conner were looking into was incredibly intriguing. I've never seen anything like it.

"Oh, and I'd pay you, of course. Double that of what your brother was making at the station!"

I bit my lip. The idea of not having to watch the little savings we had left dwindle away was nice. But, while his offer would be enough to fill the table, it was obvious how much more it would do for one of the boys.

"I'm sorry. I really don't know a lot about medicine. Perhaps I could get you in touch with John? Or James? Both would be remarkable assistance—"

"Who have not proven themselves." Barnes cut me off. "And, besides that, I'm not looking for medical knowledge. I need someone with keen eyes and a clever mind. Someone who will think outside of the box. And while I would be more than *happy* to meet the boys and help them get into the university, I wou—"

"Yes." Barnes jumped a little at my interruption and I kept speaking before he could take it back. "I accept your offer. I'll be your assistant and you'll get the boys into the university. And the pay, of course."

"Of course."

"Fantastic. Is there anything I need to sign or do?"

"For now, nothing. But I'll be back soon to start you on your first assignment."

I could hardly hold back the laugh as I ushered the professor back toward the front door and out of the house.

The Unmasked Villain

For the first time in ages, I felt like I could breathe freely. Leaning against the closed door, I let out a small giggle. "You can do this, Sarah. All that's left is for Thomas to get better."

* * *

Early the next day, the professor was knocking at the door and whisking me away. It had only taken the professor showing a letter from the constable to the officers to get us onto the crime scene. A few steps onto the stony shore, I froze. Seeing a dead body a second time was somehow worse than the first time, either because I hadn't been expecting it or because it was harder to pretend he was just asleep. I felt a bit nauseous, but that could have been the smell coming up from the Thames. While the water was beautiful, reflecting the rare bit of sunlight, the amount of junk that had been thrown into it made the area disgusting.

I covered my nose with a handkerchief. "I thought we'd be in the morgue or... something."

Professor Barnes smiled over his shoulder at me from where he was crouched over the body. "We'll learn more here on the field."

It was an older man, this time. His wrinkled face looked peaceful in death and had the same rosy cheeks as the last one, but his hands were bruised and his fingertips were bloody from where his nails had broken off. His shirt was oversized and cheap, but well taken care of—there wasn't a single mark or wrinkle on it. His pants, on the other hand, had been worn down and was covered in stains.

With a sigh, I kneeled down next to the professor. "You know, I've heard of something called cameras. They'd capture the moment so we could see the scene and not deal with the... *smells*."

"I have one, but we can't maneuver a photo." The professor reached out and carefully lifted the body up into a sitting position before shifting the shirt to reveal the man's right shoulder. "We wouldn't be able to see this."

A small gray, slightly raised "X" had been burned onto the man's skin. A small circle was just visible around the mark but what really stood out was the small hole next to it. Though it was deep, there wasn't any sign of blood or healing.

"When I examined the woman from the alleyway," Professor Barnes started, "the one with the rosy complexation, I found that she had the exact same markings on her shoulder."

"So the two are definitely related. Did they find out anything else?"

"It was as if she had drowned or suffocated. But that couldn't explain the rosiness. Or why our unidentified woman didn't show any signs of a struggle."

I leaned down and pointed at the hole. "What would cause it to look so... clean? A wound like that would bleed a lot, wouldn't it?"

"It could have been cleaned after they died..."

"But then why not clean this man's hands?"

Barnes slowly nodded. "When a person dies, their blood stops flowing. It sets after six hours, starts to clot..."

"So, this was done after that?"

"Most likely. Though, that wouldn't cause the rosiness either." He turned to me. "Do you notice anything? Any hints as to who the man is?"

"How would I—" I cut myself off and shook my head.

I couldn't see anything else on him or in the area, but I couldn't say that. I needed to provide something to the professor—to prove myself. I wracked my brain, trying to

The Unmasked Villain

think of anything. The only thing that stood out as odd or out of place was the stains on his pants.

Leaning forward, I pressed my nose to the largest spot and took a deep breath. Besides the general stink coming up from the water, there was a faint sharp but stale smell. It was a smell that I'd spent far too many nights leaning over recently.

Taking a deep breath, I reached out and started to pat him down. When I hit the front of his trousers, I couldn't help but notice a slight bump in his pocket which turned out to be a small bit of paper. The rainwater had damaged it but from the red color, it was clear that it wasn't some scrap from a book or note. On the edge, I could just make out a curled design—another thing that I'd spent too many nights seeing.

I clapped my hands together and stood up. "Why don't we continue this at one of the nearby pubs? I know just the one."

Chapter 3

Unlikely Alliance

The Endless Bottle Pub only had a few patrons sitting at the scattered tables when we walked in. They kept their heads down as they drank, half-hidden by the low light coming in from the windows. On the other side of the room, the bar was set up with a number of bottles, mugs, and ashtrays. On the wall behind, it there was a collection of bottles filled with different drinks stacked up on shelves.

Behind the counter was a short but buff man with black hair. He was facing away from the room, doing something with one of the bottles. I smiled and marched toward him.

I reached out and ruffled his hair. "Hello, James."

"Ms. Miller?" He turned around and pulled me into a quick hug. "How is everything? Is Mr. Miller...?"

"He's fine. You're welcome to come visit him at any time." I turned and pulled Barnes closer to the bar. "Let me introduce the two of you. James, this is Zachery Barnes from King's College. Professor, this is James Bullard—"

"One of the boys. I remember. It's a pleasure to meet you."

The Unmasked Villain

The two shook hands while James let out a small laugh. "The pleasure is all mine."

"Professor, I was thinking that perhaps James could help us? Like I said, he has been doing quite a lot of self-study when it comes to the body, and as you can see, he does have a good understanding of alcohol. He may be able to help us understand why that body still had a rosy complexion."

James stiffened. "Body?"

Barnes pulled out a photo from the inside pocket of his suit jacket and handed it over. As soon as he looked at it, James's eyes widened and he glanced toward me. "Why are you involved in this?"

"That's a bit of a long story. Do you recognize the man?"

"Not really. He's come in a couple of times. Would have a lot of drinks."

"What about a woman with black hair?" I asked. "She was probably well off."

He stared at me for a second before shaking his head. "That could describe a lot of different women."

"Right, of course. That was silly of me. Is there anything you can tell us about the man, then? Anything at all?"

"I think his name was Curtis? Maybe Corbin? He'd come by most nights and order a few different beers. He mostly stuck to himself. I only ever saw him talking to one or two people."

"What about drugs?" Barnes asked. "Anything like that?"

"Not that I noticed..."

"Alright." The professor clapped his hands together. "Is it alright if I take a look around?"

"Go ahead."

Barnes offered both of us a smile before turning around and getting to work. He was in the middle of rubbing his hand across the walls when James cleared his throat.

"So, you and the professor are...?"

"Coworkers, I suppose. He hired me as his assistant."

"You got a job? Ms. Miller, I told you, if you need money—"

"I will not hear it, young man. I told both you and Thomas that I would handle things and I *will*. Focus on making money for school. And, maybe, try speaking with Mr. Barnes some more?"

"I'm not sure I want to if he has you chasing after a murderer."

"We're not. We're just trying to figure out what caused the deaths to be so different."

James let out a small, almost crazed, laugh. "Because you'll definitely give up without knowing who killed those people."

All I could do was shrug. Turning to the room, I watched Barnes work. Some of the patrons had abandoned their drinks in favor of watching the professor as he began examining the vent. A couple of them were clearly teasing him, but some seemed interested in what he was doing.

"What if you don't find any leads here?"

I turned back to James. "I'm not sure. If the man drinks a lot, there's a chance he's been to other pubs. If we go around and ask others about him, we may be able to find something. Hopefully, we'll also find something out about that poor woman."

He nodded. "If the two of you come back tonight, I can point out the last person that Curtis talked to when he was here a couple of nights ago."

"Really? Thank you, James."

"Of course, Ms. Miller. I'm glad that I can help."

* * *

The Endless Bottle was completely different at night. The lamps had been turned on, lighting up the space almost as much as the people. Each of the seats was filled. From a quick glance, it was easy to see that most of the patrons were workers from the factories and docks in the area. The few women who were there were standing along the walls or at the tables closest to the doors, their hair half-up and the neckline on their bodices low.

As we walked in, a few of the men turned to stare at me, but they went back to their drinks as soon as the professor put his arm around my shoulders and pulled me closer.

When we approached the bar, James made his way toward us. His smile was far more forced than it had been in the morning—it was clearly his customer service smile. "What can I get for the two of you?"

"Two beers would be fine."

I wrinkled my nose at the professor's order but kept quiet.

"...Right away, sir." He turned away and came back a second later with two glasses in his hands. "Here we are, a beer and a mead for the lady. I know we're busy today, but you can find a seat over in the back right corner. Right over there, near the man with the long blond hair and all the jewelry."

"Ah! Fantastic. Dear—" I patted the professor's arm —"we really ought to leave this lovely young man a good tip."

James flushed. "You really don't need to..."

Barnes let out a chuckle. "No, no, I think the lady is right. You've been a great help. I'd be more than happy to leave a tip."

He placed a few coins down on the counter before pulling me off toward the table we'd been directed to. It didn't take long for us to spot the man once we knew what to look for. While he was wearing similar clothes to the other workers, the fabric was clearly of a finer quality. His entire body was adorned with gold and silver. It was clear that he was far more well-off than the rest of the patrons—possibly even more than anyone I'd ever met.

I wanted to take a second to steel myself but the professor had already sat us down before I could. The man turned, looked me over, and scoffed. He was about to turn away when I noticed his eyes land on Professor Barnes. Almost immediately, his whole demeanor shifted.

He sat up and smiled. "Evening."

"Good evening. My name's Zachery Barnes. I'm a professor of medicine at King's College and I was hoping—" The professor reached into his jacket pocket and pulled out the photo of the man—"you could answer some questions to help an investigation. Do you recognize this man?"

The man took the photo and looked it over. As soon as he realized what was on it, he went pale and forced the picture back to the professor. "Never seen him before."

"Are you sure?" I asked, leaning across the table. "Because I heard a rumor that the two of you knew each other."

The man got into my face and my eyes were drawn neck. One of the many necklaces he was wearing had a metal X wrapped in a circle as its charm. "What are you trying to suggest, Little-Miss-Skint?"

"Nothing." I fisted my hands into my skirt, trying to keep my face calm. "That's a very lovely necklace. I love the charm. May I ask where you got it?"

"I'm leaving."

All three of us stood up at the same time with the professor and I quickly blocking the door. As the man tried to push past us, I put out my arms. "Please, sir, we really do just want to—"

My head twisted to the side before the pain set in. Silence fell over the entire pub as everyone turned toward the sound of the slap. I took a deep breath, making sure that the hitch would be audible to the people around me. That small sign of distress was enough to break the spell that had come over the pub.

Everyone began to move at once. Some of the women came to my side and led me off to the side, assuring me that everything would be okay, though it was nearly impossible to make out what they were saying over the other voices yelling. In the spot I was just standing, there was a swarm of men. They'd cornered both the professor and the man, tossing both of them around.

I mentally cursed. I had expected the nearest table to stand, not all of this.

Suddenly, the pub doors flew open and a few officers came rushing in. They immediately descended on the group and began pulling them apart. The moment that anyone in the group showed any sign of resistance, the baton came out.

And all I could do was watch.

A hand landed on my shoulder and I jumped. A moment later, James was standing in front of me, blocking out the scene from across the room. "It's okay. It will be alright."

I could still hear them. I couldn't help but think that I'd made a mistake.

James pulled me toward him and I let myself fall into the hug. I stayed there for a while, doing my best to block out the sound. It took a long time, a lot longer than I would have expected, but the sound finally started to fade away.

When I pulled away, I found one of the officers hovering nearby. He was tall and imposing—his black hair and dark eyes were a mess from the fight.

"Sorry to interrupt." The officer glanced at James before holding a hand out to me. "I'm Officer Ollie Ruggles. Would you mind explaining what happened here?"

Before I could say anything, James stepped toward the officer. "'That man with the blond hair attacked this woman for no reason. He needs to be taken care of!"

The professor walked up from behind the officer. "And not just for the bar fight. From what I understand, he should also be arrested for being related to the recent string of murders."

The officer nodded. "I'll see what I can do."

I stood back, still cocooned by the working woman, the professor, and James, and watched as the man was forced out of the pub. It didn't take long for everyone else to go back to their drinks afterward, acting as if nothing had even happened despite the number of bruises and blood on their faces and arms.

Suddenly, Barnes cleared his throat. "I plan to interview the man tomorrow. If you'd rather not accompany me—"

"No." I cut him off. "I should be able to join you. I'll just... need to pull out my Sunday bests."

Chapter 4
Revelations

The door to Thomas's room opened and John looked in. His brown curls and black dress shirt were both covered in flour. Before I could say anything, he flashed me a smile and held up a basket that was filled with deformed and burnt biscuits.

"I thought I'd bring a little gift with me. Didn't think it could... go wrong."

"That's very kind of you. Will you need to stay here while you search for a new place, or was the fire damage not that bad?" I joked.

He laughed as he walked into the room. "It's fine. I made sure I had a bucket of water on hand."

I smiled and watched as he handed his father one of the biscuits. I turned to Thomas, waiting for him to say something, but he only stared at the food.

After a moment, John cleared his throat and turned to me. Even in the somewhat low lighting of the room, it was easy to see the wetness in his eyes. "Are you ready for today?"

"I think so. You know, your father used to put me

through interrogations when we were children." John sat down next to me on the bed as I continued, "Any time anything would happen around the house, he'd sit me down in the dining room and start pacing around the place. Then, after I was *thoroughly* anxious, he'd start throwing out random questions, trying to get anything to stick.

"He got smarter about it when we were older. His questions started to *actually* be about what he wanted to know. Not to mention he was able to lay some traps. Catch me up —even when I hadn't done whatever crazy thing he was trying to figure out."

"He used to do that to me too—before Mom died."

I reached out and squeezed his shoulder. "He'll get better soon."

John stared at his father, his expression shifting. Before I could pull him into a hug, his face hardened and he nodded. "He will. God will take care of him. You should get going—you don't want to be late."

"You're right." I placed a kiss to the top of both of their heads before leaving.

* * *

The eyes of every officer were on me as soon as I entered the station. I wasn't sure if it was because of what I'd done the other day or because of how dressed up I was, but all I could do was hold my head up high and keep walking.

It didn't take me long to reach the constable's office. After a few quick pleasantries, Eric escorted me down the hall to the same room that I'd been in just a few days before.

It was just as cold inside the interrogation room as before. I took my seat, this time on the other side of the table, and waited. A few minutes later, the professor was brought in. Instead of his usual tweed suit, he was wearing a very expensive silk shirt, a fitted black jacket, a jabot, and a top hat. It would only take a glance for someone to see that Professor Barnes was rich.

"Morning, Ms. Miller. How do I look?"

"Like you don't know the finer details of clothing. Jabots are more of a woman's accessory nowadays."

"I... see. Well then, let's hope that it looks better on you." He quickly untied it and moved to place it around my neck.

"It covers my necklace like this..." I considered the lacy material. It was definitely more impressive than the old pendant I had picked out in the morning. "But it's certainly more expensive. I'm sure it will be fine."

The professor turned to Constable Fear. "Well, then, I believe we're ready to get started."

"I'll tell Officer Ruggles to bring the suspect in."

The professor and I waited in silence with each second feeling longer than the last. While I did my best to stay composed, Barnes quickly took to pacing the room. By the time Ruggles came in with the man from the pub, I was worried that the professor was going to end up sweating through his jacket. It was clear that he wasn't as comfortable with the high-class image as I'd hoped.

When the man was forced into his seat, his crossed his arms and glared at the table.

"Hello, again." I leaned forward, putting on the best smile I could. "I'm sorry, but I don't think I caught your name last time."

It was only after the officer kicked his chair that the man responded. "Philip Ayers."

"Ayers, hmm? That name's familiar. Zachery, dear, do you recognize it?"

"The family's donated to King's College quite a few times."

"Ah, yes! I remember now! How is your father? He's always been so kind when we would meet up."

He looked me up and down. "Are you really trying to suggest that you know my father?"

"In passing." I held out my hand. "My name is Lady Annabelle Ev—"

Ayers began to laugh. "You're no lady."

I dropped my hand. I hadn't expected him to call my bluff. My mind raced, trying to come up with some other angle. "No, I'm not. I'm just the woman that you attacked for pointing out your necklace. You know, as the one you attacked, I'm the victim. I'm sure once the judge hears from me about how violent your crimes are, you'll face the proper punishment. What is it they give out again... Imprisonment? Corporal punishment? Or... They do still administer the death penalty, don't they?"

"Not for something like this." Ayers cut in. Even though his voice was calm, his face had gone pale.

"Hm... Well, I'm sure if I said I didn't want there to be any charges or punishment, you'd be let out of here right away..." He shifted in his seat and I turned to Barnes. "You had some questions you wanted to ask?"

"Ah, yes. Mr. Ayers, how did you know about the man from the photo?"

"Curtis was around the pub a lot so me and my friend got him a drink a few times. That's all."

"Only drinks? No other substances?"

"Nothing."

The professor nodded. "Alright. Then, can you tell me why was your necklace's pendant burned into his shoulder?"

"That's none of your business."

The Unmasked Villain

"Isn't it?" I asked. "I mean, is that not why you attacked me? I'm sure if I heard the reason behind why that necklace and branding was so important..."

Ayers let out a small laugh. "You're pushing it, lady."

"We just want to know what happened to Curtis."

"Well, I can tell you that a mark on the shoulder had nothing to do with it."

I crossed my arms. "No, but when the mark is on both of their shoulders..."

"Are you really going to start trying to blame me for Fiona?"

A small smile spread across my face. "And, who, may I ask, is Fiona?"

At my question, Officer Ruggles cleared his throat. "Fiona Donna was identified as the body uncovered three nights ago, though, I don't believe that information has been made public."

"Oh, you little—" Ayers jumped out of his seat and started to charge toward the officer.

As soon as he got within arm's reach, Ruggles grabbed his shoulder and threw him against the wall. A crunching sound filled the room and, a second later, blood started to drip down from his nose.

The officer turned and nodded his head toward the door. "If the two of you wouldn't mind..."

"Of course." Professor Barnes grabbed my arm and started to pull me out of the room. "We'll let you deal with this."

As soon as the door closed, I leaned against the wall. When the professor offered me a handkerchief, I happily took it to cover my face for a moment.

"I hadn't thought that things would take such a turn..."

"Nor did I..." The professor cleared his throat before

moving to stand in front of me. "I would like to apologize. When I asked you to assist me, I didn't realize we would be finding ourselves in the same room as a killer..."

I shook my head. "We don't know that he was the one who killed them—just that he has more information than he's letting on."

"That is... very true. Hopefully, when things calm down, we'll be able to get more out of him." He looked me up and down. "If you're still interested in being my assistant, that is. If this is too much for yo—"

"No! No. It's fine." I handed the handkerchief back to him and put on the best smile I could. The words "King's College" kept repeating in my head; there was no way I could let this opportunity go. "Once the man has calmed down, I'm sure the police will leverage his slip up and get us plenty of information to work with."

The professor nodded before turning and starting down the hallway. "I'll go get Constable Fear. He'll want to know about what happened."

I watched Barnes go for a moment before closing my eyes, trying to process everything. I'd known that my clothes weren't the most expensive, but I hadn't expected him to know that I was lying about who I was right away. I grabbed the fabric of my skirt and let out a shaky breath, trying to not think too hard about how easy it had been to threaten the man instead.

A loud thump from the interrogation room startled me out of my thoughts. Before I could even get to the door, Officer Ruggles threw it open.

His eyes went wide as soon as he saw me. "Is Professor Barnes still here?"

"He went to get the constable. Why?"

He didn't wait for me to finish my question, he just

turned and started down the hallway. Without him standing in the way, I could see what had caused the thump sound.

Philp Ayers was lying across the table, his eyes had rolled back leaving only the whites visible. His head was twitching violently as I watched his shoulders and arms joined in on the uncontrollable jerking.

A part of me wanted to run over, but my feet were frozen in place. I couldn't do anything but stare. Even when the constable and Barnes came rushing down the hall and into the room, I couldn't do anything. As Professor Barnes barked orders at the others and more and more officers came running past to help, I couldn't do anything.

All I *could* do was watch as the man I'd just talked to died.

Chapter 5

Embarrassing Evidence

For the second time in the week, I found myself sitting in the station with a blanket thrown over my shoulders. The only difference was that this time people were staring at me with pity instead of a mixture of suspicion and repulsion.

While I wanted to leave, all I could do was sit and wait. Constable Fear had already sent one of the officers to get John from the house. He'd apparently decided that I was too slow when responding to his questions about what I'd seen and determined that I wasn't fit to go home alone. He'd been halfway through getting ready to take me himself when I managed to mutter that John had the day off.

A cup was pushed into my hand and I looked up to find Officer Conner standing over me. "The constable said I should get you something to drink."

"Thank you." I swirled the water around in the cup. "How is the investigation going?"

"There isn't one right now. And if there *were*, I wouldn't be able to discuss it with you."

Conner turned to walk away, but I reached out and

stopped him. "Does that mean you know who killed Ms. Donna?"

"Who told you—" He ripped his arm away from me. "No one killed her. She died on her own, just like I said."

He started toward his desk and I quickly followed after. "Ah, yes, and I'm sure that she burned the "X" onto her own shoulder?"

"Delusional little..." He muttered. I was a second away from slapping him when he continued, "There wasn't an 'X.'"

"Yes, there was. Professor Barnes saw it. And it was on Mr. Curtis."

"I don't know about Curtis, but I do know about my own victim. There wasn't anything like that mentioned on the report. When I spoke with her family, her father told me that she was always caught up in fantasies and often overindulged. It's not a surprise that she'd have had too much of something and it killed her."

I bit my lip, trying desperately to stop myself from screaming. When I spoke, my words were rough. "You at least brought in the man who found her body and talked with him, right?"

"There was nothing to look into. Everything the man said matched with the scene—"

"You're an idiot."

I turned and stormed off to the constable's office—not caring how many people were glaring at me for my lack of manners. I knocked but didn't wait for an answer before opening the door. Inside the mostly baren room, Eric was sitting at his desk, looking over what must have been ten different stacks of paper.

He looked exhausted but still offered me a smile. "Is John here, then?"

"No, he's not. Which is good. It means that I have time to look over Ms. Donna's case."

"Sarah, you know that you can't."

"Please, *Eric*," I countered, doing my best to match how personal he was being, "I know Conner is missing something. If you'll just let me see the files, I can confirm it."

"And then?"

"You can reopen the case and get this young woman justice."

He ran a hand down his face. "Are you sure you can even handle reading these things?"

My mind flashed the three different bodies I'd seen; each one had been more horrifying than the last. It had been harder and harder to pretend they were just sleeping. Besides the knot in my stomach at the thought of those who died, there was also the chance that I wouldn't be able to understand the reports.

The constable's stare felt heavy. It would be easy to get him to look away, but doing so wouldn't put all the pieces together.

"I need to."

Eric sighed before standing up and sorting through one of the paper piles. After a while, he handed me a thin booklet. "Take all the time you need."

Opening up to the first page, I felt my stomach drop. There was a small photo attached to it and a drawing of a body, which had red markings over the chest. It was obviously the autopsy report, but most of it was hard to understand due to the messy handwriting and the words themselves. A quick glance through it, though, was enough to see that Conner was telling the truth: there was nothing about an "X" or even any sort of hole on her shoulder.

There was also a word that I didn't understand—"suffocate"—which appeared again and again. One thing I did understand was the last sentence: "It is in my professional opinion that Ms. Fiona Donna passed away due to her own actions."

The second page was easier to read, not only because the officer who wrote it had neater handwriting, but because I'd already seen it. It was the report written by the street bobby who had been told about the body. This, at least, was exactly what I had expected. It chronicled that the man had been drinking at the Endless Bottle well into the night and that, while on his way home, he noticed something strange in an alley along the way. He'd gone to try and see what it was but ended up falling over and landing next to what he realized was a body, which he claimed he reported right away.

The rest of the booklet contained a summary of two interrogations with Ms. Donna's father: one where her body was identified and the other where he went on a tirade about her actions. She had never done what he wanted her to, apparently. Any time he tried to set up a marriage or have her learn how to handle the house, she'd find some way to "sabotage" it. Even from just reading the words, and not understanding all of it, it was clear that she'd had a bad home life.

I placed the papers down on the constable's desk and sighed. Without looking up, he reached for the pages and set them on top of the pile he'd first taken it from. "How are you feeling?"

"Justified." That caught Eric's attention. He looked at me with a raised eyebrow and I took that as a sign to continue. "Not only did the person who found the body go to the Endless Pub—the same place that Curtis and Mr.

Ayers were—but it's clear that these reports are missing information."

"Sarah..."

"Just go look at Ms. Donna's shoulder or speak with the professor. Please."

He looked over his desk and the endless amount of papers. Finally, he sighed. "Her body's already been taken away, but if Barnes is interested in submitting his own autopsy, I'll take a look at it."

"Thank you."

Without wasting another second, I ran out of the office and down into the basement of the building where the morgue was. A few officers were standing inside, watching as the professor worked on Ayer's body. I felt my own stomach turn at the sight. Ayer's legs and crouch were covered by a thin white cloth, giving him some dignity in death, but that tiny act didn't help when his stomach had been cut open.

The professor looked up from where he was elbow-deep inside the man and smiled. "Ah, Ms. Miller. Are you preparing to leave for the day?"

I tore my eyes away from the scene and looked at the floor. "Not yet. I was just hoping you could possibly write a report about what you'd noticed when examining Ms. Donna. The one that the police have is... less than acceptable."

"Alright. I'll write one up as soon as I finish here." A squishing sound filled the room. "Would you be able to get me a bowl? I'd like to empty the stomach's content to examine it."

I glanced toward the others in the room, but each officer was suddenly interested in the ground, wall, or their own hands. I clenched my hand in my skirt. "Of course, professor."

My legs felt heavy as I walked over to where the bowls were next to the body. I did my best not to look as I handed it to Barnes, but that didn't stop me from hearing the sound of *something* falling into the bowl.

"It doesn't seem as if there's anything out of the ordinary... Would you like to look, Ms. Miller?"

"No, thank you, professor. I'd really rather not."

I could feel him watching me, but I didn't dare look back. "I... see. I crossed a line, didn't I? My apologies."

"That's alright. I... think I'm just going to go upstairs and wait for John, if that's alright."

"Perfectly fine. Have a good night, Ms. Miller."

I didn't respond as I turned and hurried out of the room, desperate to get away from the body as fast as possible.

Chapter 6

Race Against Time

A week had passed since the incident at the station. No more bodies had been reported and Professor Barnes hadn't shown up since that day. Without him there with me, most of the officers wouldn't give me any new information. I couldn't even go to Eric for anything as he was too caught up with the missing person cases to see me. I was just wondering about contacting the professor and asking if my reaction to Mr. Ayers's body had made him decide to reconsider me as an assistant when I opened the door to find him sitting on the steps outside my apartment.

His suit and hair were both a mess; the rain had made the fabric sag, causing him to look like a wet rat. When he turned to look back at me, the bags under his eyes and the paleness of his face made it clear that he hadn't been sleeping.

"Ah, Ms. Miller. What fantastic timing. I was just getting ready to present my theory to you."

"I see..." I bit my lip. "Sir, are you alright? You look a little... unwell..."

"Ah, yes. Thank you for the concern. I've been up the

past few nights reading. There are many fascinating studies on the effects of different chemicals on the body."

"Well, that's wonderful. I was about to go shopping." I looked over my shoulder, into the dark hallway. Thomas would stay in his room, but the idea of leaving anyone in the house with him made me feel uneasy. "If you'd like to come with me, we can discuss this more."

"Brilliant. I shall get us a carriage."

I gripped my drawstring bag tighter, suddenly aware of how light it felt. "Oh no, I'd rather walk, if that's alright."

"Are you sure?"

The rain clung to my clothes but I just smiled and reached my hand back to grab the umbrella that was leaning against the wall. I closed the door and began making my way down the path. A second later, Professor Barnes caught up to me as he struggled with his own umbrella.

Before he could say anything, I asked him a question. "What did your reading uncover?"

"Well, when I examined Ayers's mouth, I noticed that there was a trace of some white powder on his teeth. There are a number of substances that would match that description and cause seizing, such as cocaine and heroin. But, when we talked with him, he didn't show any signs of being high."

"Then, he took it after we left the room?"

"He must have. But that would have only been approximately five minutes. Whatever it was would need to be fast reacting and incredibly concentrated."

I took a second to consider what he said. "He'd have to know that taking something like that would likely kill him."

"He would have."

"I don't think he would have committed suicide, though. He was quick to anger and violent, but he obviously thought highly of himself. If he didn't, then pretending to be from a rich family wouldn't have worked as well as it did."

"Perhaps he felt caught?"

I bit my lip. "We should still keep an open mind."

"Exactly! Thank you." His pace quickened and suddenly I was the one following him. "If only the police would think the same way."

"What happened exactly?"

"They deemed Mr. Ayers guilty of the murder of both Fiona Donna and Mr. Curtis and closed the case. I'm allowed to keep conducting research on Curtis's body, but not Ayers's body or his family home—his father's order, apparently. But, without knowing anything about him or what he had access to, there's little I can do..."

"Then... we're stuck?"

"It seems so."

I nodded to myself, thinking through everything. "Alright. Well, Ayers mentioned he had a friend, right? Maybe we can ask around and see if anyone knows who that would be. James might know something, at the very least."

"Alright. It's a plan. We'll head over as soon as you're done shopping." The professor beamed at me and held out his arm for me to grab. "Shall we?"

I felt myself bristle and took a small step back. "You don't need to do that."

"Nonsense. We're colleagues! Besides, I'm sure my wife would love it if I came home with a gift for her."

At the mention of a wife, I relaxed. "I didn't know you were married."

"I am. Mrs. Elizabeth Barnes. I met her one day when there were... complications, we'll say, with a surgery. She's one of the kindest women I've ever met."

The Unmasked Villain

"She sounds very nice. I'd love to meet her one of these days."

"Well, that's good seeing as she's been dying to meet you ever since I told her about you and your brief time as an officer."

I felt myself blush. "I see. While I hate to disappoint, but I don't plan to be dressing up as a man again any time soon."

The professor stared at me for a moment before nodding. "Alright. I'll be sure to let her know. Now, let's get to the shops."

With a slight tug, Barnes started to drag me along the streets. He was walking so fast that I was barely able to stop him when we reached the butcher's shop that I needed to go to. As soon as I did, he ran us up the stairs and held the glass door open for me.

Mr. Lyle, a larger man with a bald head, stood behind the counter watching us as we walked in. Tables were placed around the shop were covered in different cuts of meat, and I found myself staring at a few of the heads that were looking lifelessly at us. The overwhelming smell of blood and rotting meat didn't help to make the shop any more welcoming.

I unhooked myself from the professor and quickly walked over to the counter. In a second, I grabbed some coins out of my purse and placed them down. "Black pudding."

Mr. Lyle moved slowly, picking up each of the coins one at a time while his eyes stayed trained on me. "Congratulations on finally finding someone. I'm sure Thomas would be happy for y—"

"I will stop you there, Mr. Lyle. I am his assistant and that is all."

"Hmm, sure."

Mr. Lyle bent down behind the counter before I could say anything. When he came back up, he threw a long sausage on the counter and cut it in half. I couldn't do or say anything as he weighed and recut the meat again and again and again. By the time he started wrapping up the sausage, it was the length of my hand.

"Is that all you're getting?"

I jumped and turned to look at the professor. His gaze was locked onto the counter and I felt my stomach get tied up in knots. Quickly, I grabbed the bag the meat had been stuffed into. "There's only two of us. It should be more than enough."

When I stepped away from the counter, Barnes took my spot. "One pig's head and a cow's shoulder, please."

Mr. Lyle smirked and I quickly turned to go to the front of the shop and out of earshot. Looking out the window, I watched the few women who were walking around on the street, rushing from place to place while cowering under their umbrellas. The one carriage on the road was moving slowly despite the drivers constantly pushing the horses to move faster.

My eyes landed on a man with brown hair and drenched clothes a little ways down the street. His movement was awkward as he made his toward the shops, as if he couldn't fully control his feet. Every once in a while he would stumble and when he smacked into the wall of one of the buildings, he turned to lean against it and slumped down. Even from such a distance, it was easy to see his chest rising and falling quickly.

My heart lurched at the sight and I found myself shaking. Why had he left the house? He shouldn't be alone on the streets. He was supposed to be resting, getting better.

I could barely feel my arms or legs. Still, I managed to move.

Outside, I ran as fast as I could. My heart was pounding in my ears. I wanted to scream but the lump in my throat prevented it.

My knees slammed against the ground as I stopped next to him and, after a second, I almost laughed. Up close, it was easy to see that it wasn't actually Thomas; the man was much older than my brother and his nose was crooked. It had just been their movements that had been the same.

Letting out a shaky sigh, I reached out and felt the pulse on the man's neck. It was erratic but I couldn't get a clear idea of how fast it was going. He turned his head toward me, his gray eyes darting around until the right one locked onto me. As his vision focused, he began swatting at the air beside me.

"Sir, are you alright?"

He spoke slowly with each word being slightly slurred, "Go. Away. Now."

"Ms. Miller!" The professor jogged up and squatted down beside me. I quickly shifted, giving him easier access to the man who was now violently squirming. "What's happening?"

"I think he was nearly drowned."

Barnes raised an eyebrow at me before nodding. "Flag down one of the carriages. We need to get this man to a hospital."

I nodded before rushing over to the road and screaming for help.

* * *

A nurse sat beside me in the waiting room. Her blue dress, apron, and cap stood out in the otherwise gray room. I could make out the sound of the professor's voice as he argued with the doctors in some other part of the building, but, beyond that, it was eerily quiet.

"Are you cold? I can get you an extra uniform if you'd like."

I shook my head. While I was freezing, the thought of returning to the hospital just to give the clothes back didn't appeal to me.

I jumped a little when she took my hand. "You did an incredibly kind and brave thing."

"Will he be alright?"

"It's..." She only hesitated for a second, but I recognized it. She would either say it was possible and to keep praying or that they were contacting a priest to say the last rites. It had happened every other time I'd been to a hospital.

"It's unlikely. Brain damage is often a life-long struggle. He may need constant care." Something in my expression caused her to frown. "Which the hospital will provide, of course, up until we find his family."

"Of course." The words sounded hollow.

After a few minutes of listening to Barnes and the doctors fighting in the other room, the nurse cleared her throat. "It's very impressive that you're working alongside a professor. Are you looking to become a nurse?"

I shook my head. "I don't like hospitals."

"Not many people do, I'm afraid."

"Ms. Miller!" I looked up to find Professor Barnes standing in the doorway. "We've been given permission to examine the man."

I mentally sighed before standing up and following after him.

Chapter 7

Twists and Turns

The man was standing in the middle of the room completely naked. His chest was heaving as if he'd been running for hours and he was obviously favoring his left side. While I hesitated to approach the man, the professor had no qualms; he immediately stepped up to the man and started examining him. While his actions were rough, he would always whisper what it was he was going to do a second beforehand to allow the man a second to prepare himself.

I cleared my throat. "The nurse said that it was brain damage."

"Most likely from oxygen deprivation." The professor gently lifted the man's head, checking his throat. "There aren't any signs of strangulation, and with the rain, if he were drowned, it would be impossible to tell."

My stomach dropped. "We should leave him to the hospital staff."

The professor slowly turned the man, allowing me to see his back. An "X" had been branded onto his shoulder.

Unlike the other two victims we'd seen, though, there was no hole.

"I noticed this when you went to get a carriage." He turned the man back around. "Open your mouth for me? Thank you."

"He's another victim..." I let out a sigh. "Which means that he's either been wandering the streets like this for a week, or Ayers wasn't the only one behind everything."

"It would make sense for there to be another person. It's unlikely he'd have been able to do all of this with a hand—"

The man suddenly grunted and started trying to back away from Professor Barnes. As he did, his one foot gave out causing him to fall. I rushed forward and grabbed him, but the action only seemed to make him more confused and scared.

"It's alright, sir. It's okay." I moved him to sit on the bed and kneeled down in front of him. "Can you tell us your name?"

He took a second before responding. "Jer...me."

"Sorry?"

"Jeremy." The professor clarified.

"Alright. Jeremy, can you tell us a bit of what happened to you?"

"I was... chos'n. And I... waited. I couldn't breathe." He turned to me, his head moving a little bit too far to the side. "I couldn't do it."

"Chosen by who?"

"God. But I failed him. I failed... I failed..."

"Alright, it's okay. You haven't failed." When he didn't calm down, I turned to Barnes. "It might be best if we give them some space."

The professor nodded. "That's fine. I think I have everything that I need."

"Are you sure? I'm sure we can keep questioning him if we just give him some time."

"Not if it agitates him. Besides, brain damage often leads to confusion and memory problems. We can't trust his answers."

My chest was starting to feel warm. "You don't know that."

"Perhaps. But I'd still rather rely on the physical, undeniable evidence."

I bit my lip and clenched my fist in my skirt. "After he's gotten a bit of care, then? When he recovers."

"It's unlikely he ever truly will."

"And why not?" I couldn't stop myself from shaking. As I was talking, Jeremy started whining. "Isn't it *your* job to help people recover from incidents like these?"

Professor Barnes frowned. "There's still a lot we don't know about the body and the brain."

I let out a bitter laugh. "So what? There's just... no hope?"

"I didn't say that."

"But you implied it." My laugh became more chaotic. "You *implied* that there was no hope. That anyone with brain damage was a lost cause."

"Ms. Miller, please, you're starting to show signs of hysteria. I know this is hard, but you need to trust that I understand this better than yo—"

Before I could stop myself, I found myself grabbing the front of the professor's coat and shaking. "Don't act like there's no hope! Don't tell me that he'll never get better!"

A small hiccup snapped me back to the present. I turned and found Jeremy curled in on himself on the bed. I dropped the professor's coat and stepped back. I tried to find something to say, but all I could do was stare at the ground.

"It's okay, Ms. Miller." The professor's smile was awkward, as was his movement when he patted my shoulder. "Why don't you step out for a second and recollect yourself?"

I glanced at Jeremy whose face was completely pale. With a sigh, I nodded. "I'm sorry."

The door closed behind me with a soft click, leaving me to just stand and wait. A few of the doctors and nurses walking by gave me a strange look and each time I wanted nothing more than to blend into the wall.

By the time Barnes came out to see me, I felt close to tears.

Before I could say anything, the professor started rambling. "I listened to his breathing and it doesn't seem as if there is any water in them, so it's likely something else caused his asphyxiation. From what I saw inside his mouth, it was different than whatever that powdery substance was that led Ayers to his death. What are your thoughts?"

I blinked, surprised at the direction of the conversation. "Oh, um, well, just because the victims didn't have the same powder as Ayers, that doesn't mean that it's not connected, does it? Ayers clearly had access to some powerful drugs—"

"But none of the victims' throats or lungs showed signs of swelling."

"Then, what, they just had no oxygen?"

The professor stared at me for a second before breaking out into a huge smile. "That's something to consider. Thank you very much, Ms. Miller."

"Of course, sir." I shifted my weight from one foot to another. "And, again, I'd like to apologize for my behavior."

He shook his head. "That's alright. I should have been more careful given your history."

I suddenly felt cold. "You know?"

"A few months ago the constable came to the hospital asking about ways to help someone who nearly drowned. He ended up telling me the whole story then. When I asked about you the other night, I recognized the name."

"I see. So you knew the entire time." My grip on my skirt tightened. "You knew about Thomas and his brain damage and you're still sure that there's no real hope of recovery."

"I assumed that your doctor would have told you as much."

My body started to shake and I needed to take a few deep breaths before I could even say anything. "Good night, professor."

I was halfway down the hall when I felt a hand on my shoulder. "Ms. Miller... Did I say something wrong?"

I refused to turn around and look at him. "It's fine. I just... need some time to collect my thoughts."

"Alright. Well, if I did say something, I'm sorry. I know I'm not the best with these sort of things. I'll... be at the station for the rest of the night. If you need me after, I'll be at my office at the college doing research. If you'd like to talk, feel free to come anytime."

I shrugged his hand off of my shoulder. "I understand. I'll... see you tomorrow, sir."

Without looking back, I made my way to the front desk of the hospital. The nurse offered me a smile and began talking about the latest news as I waited for one of them to gather my things. I barely heard them. I didn't even bother to say goodbye once they finally handed me my purse and umbrella.

I'd made it halfway to the exit when I realized I was

missing something. Turning back around, I forced a smile for the nurse. "Sorry, was there any blood sausages with my stuff? I was doing some shopping when all of this happened."

"No, I don't believe so."

I mentally cursed, trying to remember if I'd had the bag in my hand when I called the carriage. I'd been panicked when I'd run out of the shop and, when I reached Jeremy, I... had nothing. "I see. Thank you."

Leaving the hospital, I looked around. It was getting darker and by the time I made my way back, none of the shops would be open. The only way I could get food would be if I went to the pub. As I started to walk, I tried to convince myself that I'd have the time to drink one glass of mead, even though I knew I'd probably end up having a lot more.

Chapter 8

Deceptive Clues

I was halfway through the third cup of mead when a man leaned against the bar next to me. His blond hair had a slight curl to it that was barely managed by the pig fats that he was excessively using to keep it pushed back. He smirked at me, even as I did my best to ignore him.

"What's got you down?" I took a long sip of my drink. While I was sure that he'd go away soon, my confidence fell when he threw an arm over my shoulder. "Come on. If you open up, I might be able to help."

I shrugged his arm off of me. "I'm not interested."

"Ah, but, ma'am, you don't know what I do."

He went to move his arm back around me, only for someone else to reach out and stop him. James cleared his throat as he forced the man away from me. "She said that she wasn't interested. Perhaps you'll have better luck somewhere else."

The blond-haired man immediately stiffened. With a curt nod, he turned and hurried away into the group of patrons at the bar. It didn't take long for him to find a seat next to a depressed, drunken man.

As soon as it was clear that he wouldn't be back, James turned back to me. "*Are* you okay, Ms. Miller?"

"I'm alright, James. You don't need to pity me."

"The only pity you'll get from me will be tomorrow when John finds out you're hungover and practically breaks your door down."

I let out a small laugh. "That's one way to motivate me to stop drinking."

"Another way to get you to stop drinking would be for you to talk about your problems."

I swirled the golden liquid around in its mug. Even half drunk, I knew that I couldn't tell James about the visit to the hospital; the boys were already worried enough about Thomas without having to deal with my own feelings of hopelessness thrown into the mix. With how smart the two of them were, they'd probably already figured out that the damage to Thomas was permanent anyway.

I took another long sip of the mead. "I left my shopping at the butchers."

"Really?" James shook his head. It was obvious that he knew there was more to it, but that he respected me enough not to push. "Okay. First thing tomorrow, I'll head over and buy you and Thomas a feast."

"Don't you dare."

"I will." He placed a hand on my shoulder and used the other to push the mead away from me. "You and Mr. Miller fed me more times than I can count when I was a child even though you didn't have to. Let me return the favor."

"We didn't do it to have you two waiting on us. We did it because you were John's friend."

He sighed. "Then what if John and I come over for dinner tomorrow? You know we're absolutely rotten in the kitchen."

The Unmasked Villain

"That's true. John brought by these horrible biscuits the other day. But, at least he remembered to add flour."

"In my defense, I did that when I was ten. And it's a mistake I promise I'll never make again." He moved my arm over his shoulder and started to move toward the door. "Now, come on. Let's get you home."

"No, no. You need to finish your shift!"

"It ended an hour ago. Besides, I don't think anyone would frown on me walking my moth—" He cleared his throat—"a woman home."

I bit my tongue to stop myself from saying anything. We walked down the street in silence until I finally felt composed enough to say something. "You and John should go to the professor and become his assistants."

He frowned. "So, something did happen. He didn't try anything with you, did he?"

"No, no. He has a wife." James huffed and I gave him a light slap before continuing. "I'm the one who messed up. I sort of... yelled at him."

"I'm sure he deserved it."

"He really didn't. I *was* becoming hysterical..."

James laughed—his tone bitter. "And I'm sure he caused it."

"He is a good man. And there's a lot he can do for you and John..."

He stopped abruptly and I almost fell over. When I turned to look at him, he was frowning. "You don't need to worry about that, Ms. Miller. I... already have some plans put into place. And I'm sure John does too. So, just focus on doing what you want and being happy—no matter what others might think or what it takes."

I let out a sigh, remembering the moment that I'd told the boys those exact words. It had been two years after

John's mother died and I'd moved in. They were sitting at the table while I cooked. And then they asked why I wasn't married. The mutton had burned by the time I finished explaining what a spinster was and that I was *more* than happy to claim both meanings of the term.

"I didn't know you still remembered that."

"Of course I do. It was... inspiring."

A silence fell over us for the rest of the walk. By the time we reached the front door, my head no longer felt so misty. "Thank you."

"Is it alright if I come in? I want to check on Mr. Miller."

"I'm sure Thomas would like that."

Inside, we went right up to his room. As the door clicked open, I could hear sobbing. Panic stabbed through my chest and I ran over to the closet lamp to light it. With the lights on, it was easy to see him sitting up, his arms wrapped around his stomach as he curled in on himself. A spot of maroon was slowly growing on his right shoulder.

Sitting at the edge of the bed, I pulled back his shirt to reveal a small bandage had been placed on his shoulder and had already bled through. Red stained my fingers as I removed it. The cloth hit the floor with a small splat. Without the bandage, the blood started to run down his back.

I pulled at my sleeve, ripping the fabric off. As I wiped the blood away, my stomach turned. Though it kept bleeding, I could make out two deep slashes forming an "X." I pressed the fabric to his shoulder and put as much pressure on it as I could.

"James, go to the station and get the constable. As fast as possible." He didn't respond right away; he just stared at the X. "James! Please!"

"Right."

The Unmasked Villain

He left the door open as he ran through the house. Turning back to Thomas, I began running my free hand up and down his arm. "It's okay, Thomas. It's going to be okay."

* * *

By the time the constable came back from searching the house, Professor Barnes had finished cleaning up and wrapping the cuts. Eric scanned the room, looking at James, Barnes, and myself one-by-one before clearing his throat. "Could Thomas have done this to himself?"

"No," I insisted. "There wasn't anything sharp in the room when I left. And even if he did get something, he wouldn't have been able to do that. His hands shake too much."

"So, someone broke into the house?" James's voice was shaky.

"There wasn't any sign of a break-in on any of the doors or windows."

"Well, they had to. I locked the door!" I turned to Barnes. "Didn't I?"

He bit his lips. "I don't remember you doing so."

"Then... whoever it was was just able to walk right in?" My stomach dropped. "I... I'm partly to blame for this."

"No," James argued. "The person who came in caused this. Not you."

Thomas sniffed, drawing everyone's attention toward him. When he looked up at me, he looked devastated. "J'hn."

I forced a smile onto my face. "Don't worry, he's okay. James, would you go and get him? He should be at his apartment."

As he left the room, I made my way over to the wardrobe and took out a new shirt. The other two watched me as I slowly worked with Thomas to get him changed—the cuts making it take longer than usual.

Once Thomas was settled, Constable Fear stepped forward. "Has anyone been stalking you or your family?"

"Not that I've noticed."

"What about grudges against Thomas? Or any changes in behavior from those around him? Any details could help."

"Well, the person the professor and I have been inadvertently trailing, who just seems to *love* putting an "X" on people's shoulders, might have something to do with it!"

Eric rubbed his nose and looked away from me. "Mr. Ayers is dead."

"And clearly he had an accomplice! Or a copycat!"

"I'd say this is the latter," the professor pipped up. "The others were branded, not cut. Whoever did this didn't know all the details."

"No one should know any details. We haven't released that to the news—just the identities we could find. The papers don't even know that we've reopened the case."

It felt like every part of my body froze. "But the other officers do. That's why the autopsy didn't include the mark that Ms. Donna had. And, if they did that, then Mr. Ayers..."

"Might have been murdered," the constable finished for me as he sat down on the chair next to the bed. "God, please, let it just be an accomplice."

Professor Barnes reached out and patted Eric's back. As he did, we made eye contact. The look on his face made it clear what he thought; the station wasn't as safe a place as we wanted to believe.

Chapter 9

Hidden Motives

In the kitchen, I pulled open cupboards to try and find anything I could to make for the constable and the professor. The two of them had helped Thomas down the stairs and taken a seat in the parlor, where they'd started talking about *something*. Their voices were too quiet for me to hear, but I could occasionally make out mine and Thomas's names. A part of me wanted to storm in there and demand to be included, but I knew that I was too tired and emotionally drained. If I were to join in, I'd end up having a breakdown during the discussion.

After a while, I finally managed to find something—a few tea leaves—and quickly started focusing on going through the different motions. It was somewhat therapeutic. By the time I finished making the drinks and joined the pair of them, they'd stopped whatever conversation they were having.

When I sat down, the constable cleared his throat. "Sarah, the two of us have been talking, and we think that it may be best for you and Thomas to move out of your home for a while."

I grabbed one of the tea cups and let the warmth from it seep into my hands. "The boy's apartments aren't big enough."

"Your parents?" Barnes asked.

"They died when we were young."

Eric cleared his throat. "I can speak with my wife. I'm sure she wouldn't mind."

"I appreciate the offer, but I doubt Thomas can handle being in the same place as a baby. It would be too loud."

"Then," the professor chimed in, "I suppose you'll have to move into my place."

"Your wife—"

"Won't mind at all. Like I said, she's been dying to meet you!"

I opened my mouth to say something, but the constable beat me to in. "If she doesn't feel comfortable with it, we can find you both a room somewhere *with* the station covering the cost. Either way, it would be best to pack up what you need right away."

After a second, I nodded. "Alright. I'll start now."

It didn't take long to gather my own stuff into a bag; most of the fabrics, tools, and books that I had hadn't been touched in months. I ended up spending most of my time packing in Thomas's room. I went over each of his books and outfits carefully, trying to figure out what combination would make him happiest but I had no real clue.

I finished gathering everything and turned to take a quick glance around. Even from the door, the splotches of red on the bedding stood out. The idea of leaving it there for who knew how long made me sick. Placing the bags in the hallway, I moved over and carefully removed the bedding. It didn't take long to replace them, but when I reached down

The Unmasked Villain

to gather the sheets off the floor, I caught a glimpse under the bed.

There was a wooden box that I'd never seen before hidden away in the far corner. It took a couple of attempts, but I finally managed to reach it. The wood was a dark oak and the golden latches had a slight shine to them, but what really stood out about it was the lack of dust. While I'd done my best to keep Thomas's room clean, I was sure that I'd forgotten to sweep under the bed.

Opening the lid, I found myself staring at ten different vials. While three were empty, the others contained either a white powder or a clear liquid.

Slamming it shut, I ran down the stairs with the box held close to my chest. The constable and professor looked up at me as I entered the room but I walked right past them and crouched down in front of my brother. "Thomas, what is this?"

He slowly turned to look at the box. When his vision finally focused, he jerked back in his seat with a whimper. "No."

"Is it yours?"

He shook his head—the action jerky.

"But you recognize it?"

He hummed.

"Where did it come from?"

He caught my eye and for a second, I felt like I was back to when we were children; him standing next to me as we faced down our father's scolding. I'd always been the one to disappoint him, but Thomas would stay by my side; he never told on me.

I let out a sigh and placed the box on the table for the other two to see. "This isn't ours. It was under his bed. And, whoever left it there... I think Thomas knows them."

The two crowded around the box and opened it. While the constable immediately ran a hand through his hair, the professor reached out and uncorked one of the liquid vials. He sniffed it and then did the same thing to one of the powdered ones.

"I can't be sure, but I believe they're stimulants—drugs meant to provoke activity."

Eric took the vials from the professor and placed them back in the box. "Do you know anyone who would have access to drugs like these?"

"Only the professor here."

"What about James or John?" Barnes asked. "From what you've said, they're interested in the topic."

"But they don't have the money for it."

"We'll still need to question them." Thomas and I both let out a sound of protest at the constable's words. "I'm not saying that it's them, just that they might have more information about the box or how it got there."

"Alright. I understand."

"Ms. Miller, have you noticed any changes in your brother?" the professor suddenly asked. "How alert he's been or active?"

I turned to stare at Thomas only to find him already looking at me. "He does seem a little more present, though there are still bad days. But, that's normal, right? He's meant to be recovering."

"Fascinating." The professor stood up and moved to stand over Thomas. He reached out to grab his face, but I swatted it away. "Please, Ms. Miller, I just need to check his pupils."

"Why? Do you think he's been taking drugs while I wasn't looking?"

"He may have been given them, yes."

The Unmasked Villain

I was speechless. I watched as Professor Barnes moved a finger past my brother's face a few times. When he stepped back, he turned to the constable. "It doesn't seem like he's been given a dosage recently, but he should still be monitored.

My stomach dropped. "There were three vials missing. Do you think he was given them all at once?"

"No. If they did then he'd have likely died."

"So, whoever it is has been in my house *multiple* times?"

The constable stood up and clapped his hands together, capturing our attention. "Alright, professor, take a taxi with Thomas and Sarah to the hospital. Tell them to check and monitor Thomas. After that, take Sarah to your home, get her set up, and then come back here.

"In the meantime, I'll guard the house. When the boys get here, I can tell them where you went, then send them to get interviewed. Once the professor comes back, I can go back to the station and set up patrol to watch over all of you."

Barnes nodded. "I'll go wave down a carriage."

As soon as he was gone, Eric turned to me. "Where did you leave your bags?"

"The hallway, but I can—"

"Let me. Just focus on Thomas."

In a second, the two of us were left alone in the parlor. I sat down and took Thomas's hand. The floorboards squeaked above us, but besides that, the room was completely silent. It was strange to think that someone could have been here, walking around, doing whatever they wanted, and I had no idea.

"Please, Thomas, just tell the officers what you know."

He leaned over and rested his head against my shoulder. "L've you."

"I love you, too." I squeezed his hand before resting my head on top of his. I gave myself thirty seconds to just *be*. When it passed, I pulled Thomas closer to my side and forced the two of us up.

I guided us out of the parlor, down the hall, and to the front door where Professor Barnes was waiting for us. It took a while to slip Thomas into the carriage, but by the time we did, the constable had come out with our bags.

Eric slammed the carriage door shut and I turned to look out the window as the house grew further away. My chest tightened and I found myself needing to turn away. The professor caught my eyes and smiled. I knew it was meant to be comforting but the stiffness in his jaw just made it clear how awful everything was.

I closed my eyes and let my head lean back against the chair. Before long, I ended up falling asleep.

Chapter 10

Closer to Home

Professor Barnes woke me up when we reached the hospital so I could help him escort Thomas inside. The entire experience went by in a blur—the only thing that I remembered afterward was the staff leading my brother into a room and the nurse from earlier in the day promising me that they'd take good care of him.

Before I knew it, we reached the professor's house. A metal fence was set up around a beautifully maintained yard filled with flowers. The building itself was just as stunning. A bit of ivy was crawling up the red bricks, framing the windows. In the middle of it all, a black front door stood out, acting like a beacon.

We'd only just stepped out of the carriage when an older woman came charging out of the house. Her hair was pulled back into a braided bun making it easy to see the gray streaks mixed in with the black. The green dress she was wearing didn't fit her well. The fabric was tight against her shoulders but hung a little too much near her waist.

As soon as Barnes saw the woman, he smiled and jogged toward her.

"My dear! Let me introduce you to my assistant, Ms. Sarah Miller. Ms. Miller, this is my wife, Elizabeth Barnes."

She reached out and grabbed my hand. "It's good to finally meet you!"

"Likewise."

"Now." Mrs. Barnes turned to her husband. "May I ask what's in the bags?"

"Ah, yes, they're Ms. Miller's things. See, she's going to be—"

Mrs. Barnes raised her hand, effectively silencing her husband. She turned to me and smiled. "It seems like a long explanation and you look absolutely exhausted. Why don't I take you to our guest room, let you get settled in while I make you something to eat? Then, you can explain everything to me."

"That... sounds nice."

"Excellent. Zachery, please unload the carriage and leave the man a good tip, yes?" Before Barnes could respond, Mrs. Barnes took me by the arm and started to lead me inside. As soon as we were a distance away, she began whispering to me, "I'd like to apologize for my husband. He's quick to get excited and forgets to ask permission before doing things."

"Oh, no. He's been very kind."

She hummed. "He really is. Kind, that is."

The inside of the house was just as beautiful as the outside. The red walls were covered in a variety of paintings with some depicting landscapes and flowers. Bookshelves seemed to line almost every wall and even then they still didn't seem to have room for all of them. We walked past what looked like a parlor, a dining room, and a kitchen before reaching the stairs and going up.

My mouth fell open when we reached the guest room.

The Unmasked Villain

The place looked like it belonged to the queen herself. A four-poster bed was placed in the middle of the room and was covered in golden-colored sheets with at least six pillows. There was a window with a writing desk underneath it that was already set up with papers, quills, ink pots, and even a vase of flowers and on the ground was a long, soft creme rug.

I walked over to the bed and sat down. When I finished taking it all in, I found Mrs. Barnes watching me from the door. "Have you had anything to eat today?"

"Oh, you don't have to worry about me."

"I'll take that as a no, then. I'll be back soon. Oh, and feel free to get changed into something more comfortable once Zachery brings you your things."

A second later, she was rushing down the hallway. With nothing else to do, I fell back onto the bed and took a deep breath. If I strained my ears, I could just make out the sound of people walking around.

A knock came from the door and I quickly sat up. "Come in."

The professor poked his head in and raised one of the bags up to show me. "Here you are. All of your things."

"Thank you."

"Of course." He hesitated for a moment, his eyes darting between the door and the bags. "Would you like me to help you unpack?"

"No, that's alright."

"Well then, I'll head back to your place and let Constable Fear know that everything went smoothly."

With a final nod, Barnes turned and left.

Before I could get comfortable there was another knock. "Sarah? Are you decent?"

"Oh, uh, yes, Mrs. Barnes."

The door opened and I was immediately hit by the smell of different spices and butter. As she walked into the room, I could see the platter she was holding. There was a bowl filled to the brim with some brown soup, a plate filled with Yorkshire puddings, a boiled egg, and even some kind of tart.

"You didn't get changed?"

I forced my eyes away from the tray. "Oh, no. I quite like this dress."

"I can understand that. It's very pretty. I wish I could wear something like that, but they don't make basques for woman like me."

"Well, they should. If you want, I can make you something."

She let out a small laugh and sat down beside me, placing the tray between us. "I appreciate it. When Zachery mentioned that he misunderstood the police officer thing... Well, I admit, I was slightly worried about how the meeting would go."

"I can hardly judge anyone for not being like everyone else."

"I see. Thank you." She let out a small chuckle. "Well, we don't need to get into all of that. Why don't you tell me about what happened?"

While I'd originally only planned to tell her about the case, something about Mrs. Barnes made it easy to talk about everything. I told her about Thomas's accident, taking care of him for months, and seeing that the station was looking to replace him. I mentioned trying to take his place so that he had something to go back to when he finally got better, only to fail and end up falling into whatever was going on with these bodies marked with an "X." And finally, finding out someone

The Unmasked Villain

had been breaking into my home and drugging my brother.

When I finished, Mrs. Barnes handed me a handkerchief. "I'm sorry to hear all of that. But, at least the day's done and can't get worse."

"If I'm honest, I was planning on heading over to the station in a bit. Check on the boys."

"Alright. I'll get a carriage for us."

"Oh, you don't need to—"

"Do you know how far the station is from here? Or how to get there?" When I didn't respond, she stood up. "That's what I thought. I'll go get that carriage ready for us."

* * *

The station was a mess when Mrs. Barnes and I walked in. People were yelling and running around and at the center of it all was the constable. While he'd been struggling to stay composed at the house, he looked totally ragged now. He locked eyes with me and his face paled.

He rushed over to meet us. "Ms. Miller, I thought you were at the professor's house?"

"I was. Mrs. Barnes and I came here to see the boys after you're done with them."

The constable cursed under his breath. "It may not be that simple. John admitted to the crime."

"Pardon?" A rough laugh forced itself out of me. "You don't really think that he could have done that, do you?"

"You did say that Thomas likely knew whoever had been giving him the drugs."

"But that... John is his *son!*" I started grasping at the fabric of my dress. I could feel everyone's eyes on me after my outburst, but it didn't matter. "Let me talk to him."

"Sarah—"

"No, Eric, please. I need to... I just need to convince him to tell the truth."

He sighed. "He's in holding—"

I didn't wait for him to continue before I ran past him. The interrogation rooms had been cold, but the holding cells beyond them were even worse. Besides the freezing temperatures, the area was filled with the smell of urine and was incredibly dark. I would have missed the boys entirely if it weren't for John's voice.

"Auntie?"

I twirled around and ran over to the bars on one of the cells. Inside the small space stood John, by himself, shaking. "Oh, dear, are you okay? What happened? They said you claimed you were the one to hurt your father?"

"I... I did."

"No, no, sweetie. I think there was a misunderstanding. Someone broke into the house and they—"

"Cut an 'X' into his right shoulder." My stomach dropped at his words. "I... I just... I figured if he was a Chosen, then God might help him."

"What do you mean?"

"If you submit, he'll send you signs. Sometimes you see things, other times you'll feel or hear them." He let out a shaky breath. "He told me that I could help Father."

"John?"

"I was chosen. He accepted me. See!" He turned around and I could just make out him moving the collar of his shirt down. It was too dark to see any details, but I knew what was likely there: an "X" burnt into his skin. "He accepted me, and he'll help Father. I-I know he will."

Chapter 11

Breaking Barriers

I stood against the office's wall beside Mrs. Barnes as the professor and the constable circled each other. Both of them were ranting while completely ignoring the other in favor of their own argument. One of them was saying something about cults and monitoring while the other was talking about gathering everyone they could and trying to control the situation.

I couldn't really make out the finer details of what they were saying. Their voices sounded distant. My eyes couldn't focus either. Everything looked slightly blurred. Even my body felt wrong; it seemed both too big and too small.

When I made out "John" and "prosecuted," it felt like someone had thrown water at my face.

"No." Everyone in the room turned to look at me. "You can't."

Eric shook his head. "I'm sorry, Sarah. I can't even begin to imagine how stressful this is for you, but we need to control the situation as quickly as possible."

"And arresting him will do that? Why not just... question him? Try and figure out who put those stupid ideas into his head?"

"We will be, but we also need to keep him here—"

"Why?"

"Because he committed a crime."

I wanted to scream.

Professor Barnes cleared his throat. "If I may, if we do let him go, we can monitor him—see where he goes, who he interacts with—"

"No," the constable interrupted. "Doing that not only risks him telling the others that we're investigating them but also puts John in danger. If they decide that he's a liability..."

I didn't hear the rest of his sentence. My whole body felt like it was in a haze. I barely felt the land on my shoulder when Mrs. Barnes approached.

She glared at both men in the room. "Why don't we focus on getting as much information as we can *first* before jumping to any conclusions."

After a moment, the constable turned and opened the door to his office. "Conner! Come here for a moment."

It didn't take long for the officer to reach the room. He stood up straight and only spared a second to glare at me. "Sir."

"We're going to be interrogating John Miller right away. Get ready for it."

"And," Barnes cut in, "will we be able to sit in?"

"No. I'm sorry, but with it being John... Only those assigned to the case will be able to be a part of the interrogation."

I stood up straighter as I thought about his words. "Alright. Thank you, Eric."

I quickly marched out of the room, doing my best to not look too excited as I made my way toward the interrogation

The Unmasked Villain

rooms. When I was joined by Conners a minute later, I gave him a small curtsy—an action that clearly made him angry.

"What are you doing here?"

"I'm here because the constable requested it. I was one of the people originally assigned to the case."

"You're not an officer."

"No, but he didn't *say* officers." When his expression didn't change, I shifted my approach. "I just want to be sure we follow everything to the letter so that there are no problems later on."

His eye twitched. "You wouldn't have come in pretending to be your brother if that were true. Do you know how many cases you could have messed up?"

I pushed down the urge to point out I was right about the case being a murder. "You're right. It was lucky that I was paired with someone who could compensate for my blunder."

"You were." With a nod, Conners opened the door. "You don't say anything, alright? You're just here to make sure that the paperwork stays consistent."

"Of course."

I hurried into the room before he could change his mind or go check with the constable. Once inside, I positioned myself so that I would be able to see John as soon as the door opened. After a few minutes of waiting, he was shoved inside.

His clothes had become wrinkled and his hair was a mess. Even though he was holding himself up straight, it was easy to see the slight tremor that had taken over his hands. A part of me wanted to run up and hug him, but I knew that doing so would get me kicked out. I had to just bite my tongue and watch.

When John tried to meet my eyes, I had to look away.

"Please say your name and occupation."

John turned to Officer Conner. "John Miller. I'm... Well, I just work odd jobs at the moment. Anywhere that needs a hand and will give money."

"And, you admit that you went into your father, Thomas Miller's, home and severely injured his shoulder?"

"I did." He turned to look at me. "But I didn't do it out of malice. I just wanted him to get better."

"And how would carving an 'X' into his back do that?"

"Not his back, the right shoulder—the place of honor. It's given to those who are chosen. It makes them able to know His will. I figured, if he had God's favor, God would help him get better."

"I see. And do you know a Ms. Fiona Donna?"

"No."

"What about Curtis Waters? Jeremy Graves?"

John jumped a little at Jeremy's name. "Brown hair and broken nose? He's the one who first told me about everything and helped me become Chosen."

"When was this?"

"I met him about two months ago, outside the Endless Bottle. We've been meeting up at the shops ever since." My stomach dropped. I'd had no idea that that had been happening. "He... listened to me. About everything. After a while, he started to tell me about the visions he'd seen. And then, about a week ago, he told me that He told him I was ready.

"He gave me something to drink and then, the next thing I knew, I woke up in a room. I heard Him. And then, I was given the choice. I could turn away, or get the mark to prove I was Chosen."

"And that led you to cutting up your father's shoulder?"

"I didn't want to. But, He told me that my father would

get better if he got marked. Jeremy was supposed to help with the ceremony earlier today, but... he never showed up. So... I had to do it myself."

"And the drugs?"

John looked between Conner and I. "What drugs?"

"The ones that had been hidden in your father's room and been given to him. That he's currently in the hospital recovering from."

John's face lost all color and he was jumping out of his seat. "Is he alright? What was he given? Do they know?"

"Well, I don't know what it was but I'd imagine you do. Since you gave it to—"

"I didn't! I'd never!" His eyes landed on me. "You have to believe me."

Before I could reassure him, Officer Conner spoke up. "If you didn't do it, who did?"

He shook his head. "I don't know."

"I'm sure you don't. Why don't we give you a minute alone? Maybe then, you'll have a better memory."

Conners turned toward the door and I knew I was supposed to follow him but my legs were shaking too badly. I'd just taken a deep breath to calm myself down when John grabbed my hand. His face looked gray and his eyes were sunken in. If it weren't for his ragged breaths, it would be easy to think he was dead.

"I'm sorry. I just... He said that it would make Father better."

I lost all composure and pulled him into a hug. He started crying into my shoulder and I found myself running my hand through his hair. A thousand different words come to mind, but none of them seemed right. Pulling back, began rubbing his arms. "It's going to be okay. I promise. I-I need to go now, but... it will be alright."

I waited just long enough for John to nod at me before making my way out of the room. A few of the officers watched me as I walked through the station, but I kept my head up. Outside, the Barnes were loitering around the street, looking back and forth. When the professor spotted me, he grabbed Mrs. Barnes's arm and started leading her toward me.

"Ms. Miller, there you are! We've been looking everywhere for you."

"My apologies. I wanted to be sure that I got to the interrogation as soon as possible."

"You got in?" Professor Barnes laughed. "Brilliant! Fantastic work. What did you learn?"

Mrs. Barnes cleared her throat. "It might be better to discuss this as we head back home. It's late and... well... I'm not sure the constable will be happy if he learns what you did."

She wrapped her arm around my own and started to lead me away from the station. By the time we'd gotten into the carriage, I'd managed to tell them about the names of the victims, that they believed they were chosen and given signs by God, and that John had carved the "X" to try and save Thomas too.

"Interesting... It sounds like they were facing different kinds of hallucinations. But why take him to a secondary location?"

"Well, we may be able to find out more." When both of them turned to look at me, I shifted slightly in my seat to sit straighter. "We know that the man from the shore, Curtis, was at the Endless Bottle. That's where we found Ayers and is now where we know Jeremy was when he... *converted* John. So, if we want to learn more, we'll need to go get a drink."

Chapter 12

Desperate Measures

We'd spent the rest of the carriage ride back to the Barnes's house discussing how to best approach the situation. It was obvious that going to the Endless Bottle and asking around about how to become "chosen" wouldn't be the safest course of action—especially not alone.

Before we could figure out all the details, the carriage slowed to a stop. When Professor Barnes reached for the door, it was suddenly forced open from the outside by Officer Ruggles. His frame blocked us in the carriage as his eyes darted around, taking us in. After a moment, he nodded and stepped back.

"I'm glad to see you three are safe."

The professor frowned. "Why wouldn't we be?"

"I wasn't sure when I saw that symbol on the door..."

"What?"

The Barnes couple pushed past the officer and ran over to their home. From their reaction alone, I could tell it was bad. While Barnes immediately started pacing around the garden, Mrs. Barnes became rigid. I hurried over to them but stopped at the lawn's fence.

It was hard to see from how dark the wood was and the time of night, but an "X" had been carved into the middle of the door. The only reason that I even noticed it was because of the paper stabbed into the door above it. Different letters had been glued to spell out the word "stop." I slowly walked up to it and ran my hand over the "X." The lines were wide but shallow. Whoever had done it had clearly spent a while carving the wood to make it appear perfect.

I was started out of my thoughts when Officer Ruggles cleared his throat behind me. "I saw it when I first arrived. When I knocked and no one answered, I was worried that something had already happened."

I nodded. "Did you look around the outside of the house? Did they get inside?"

"It didn't look like it."

"Alright, then..." The professor turned and reached for Mrs. Barnes's arm. "We're going to go inside where it's safe. Officer, you're more than welcome to join us."

"No. I should probably stay out here."

The professor barely waited for Officer Ruggles's answer before ushering us inside. As soon as the door was closed, he ran ahead of the two of us and began lighting every lamp he could. When he disappeared around a corner, I turned to Mrs. Barnes.

It was clear that she had relaxed somewhat now that we were inside, but she didn't stop staring forward aimlessly. I shifted in front of her and smiled. "How about I go and make us some tea?"

"No thank you, dear," Mrs. Barnes whispered. "It's far too late for anything like that. It's probably best if all of us go and get a few hours of sleep."

The Unmasked Villain

"Of course. Is... there anything I can do for you before that?"

She shook her head. "I'll just... talk to my husband once he's calmed down some. I'll see you tomorrow at breakfast."

With that, she left me alone in the hallway. I took one final look at the door to make sure that it was locked before going up to the guest room. It didn't take long for me to get changed and prepare for a night of pretending to sleep.

* * *

The table in the dining room was covered in a wide spread of food. Plates with ham and cheese littered the table and bowls of porridge were set up at three of the six seats with tiny saucers of fruits, honey, and milk. There were just as many drinks to choose from with there being pitchers filled with water, whisky, and orange juice.

Based on how Mrs. Barnes looked from her seat at the center of the table, she'd been up most of the night cooking. The professor, who was sitting beside her, didn't look much better. He was still wearing the same suit as he was the night before and a bit of stubble had already started to form on his chin.

As soon as I sat down, Barnes cleared his throat. "Ms. Miller, I would like to thank you for your work so far and I would appreciate it if you would remain in the position as my assistant."

"Of course, I'll continue helping."

"Fantastic. Then, I'll be returning to the college tomorrow and start doing some planning. When I get back, I'll tell you about our next project."

I leaned forward in my seat. "Sorry? What do you mean next project?"

"For all of our safety, I have decided that we will be leaving the rest of this investigation to the police."

"We can't do that."

"Ms. Miller—"

"No! How can we turn our back on these people? On Thomas and John?"

"The police—"

"Don't know anything! They didn't even realize they were murders! And we've already discussed how it's possible that it's likely whoever is doing this is tied to the police in some way! If we just abandon this now, we may never get answers."

"I understand. And under any other circumstance, I would never pull back in the middle of research. But, this is a direct threat to us and your brother too, once he gets released from the hospital. I made this decision and it's final."

I stared at him for a moment, barely able to stop myself from shaking. When I finally calmed down slightly, I stood up. "I understand. If you'll excuse me, I'm not feeling well."

I was going through my things in my room when Mrs. Barnes walked in. The two of us stared at each other, waiting for the other person to start speaking. After a few minutes, she sighed and bowed her head.

"I'm sorry about how things have turned out."

"It's alright. I understand."

"We only want to keep you safe."

A bitter laugh forced its way out of me I could barely hold back a sob. When Mrs. Barnes pulled me into a hug, I realized that I was once again shaking. She started muttering something as she pet my hair, but I couldn't make it out. My mind was too focused on the image of blood pouring out of an "X" on my brother's shoulder and my nephew standing behind bars with the same damned mark burned into his skin.

After the tears stopped, I found myself just staring. I knew that I couldn't put the Barnes through the same thing, but the idea of leaving it in the hands of someone else didn't sit right either.

"I think I need some time on my own..." I licked my lips, trying to find some way to ask for what I needed. "Would you happen to have any old clothes that you don't need anymore? I think I'd like to just do something with my hands and—"

"There's no need to explain. I have some clothes that will *never* be worn again in my old closet." She got up and started toward the door. Before she left, though, she turned back to me with a nervous look on her face. "I... hope you don't mind that they're for men?"

I mentally cursed—I hadn't wanted to dress up as a man again. "That's fine. I'll take anything I can get at this point."

Eight hours later, I found myself slipping out of the household, keeping my head down as I passed Officer Ruggles, with a large bag over my shoulder and a pair of loose-fitting brown trousers under my skirt. The binding felt just as uncomfortable as it had when I was pretending to be Thomas, but I focused on my breathing.

The Endless Bottle was much further away from the Barnes's house than I was used to walking. By the time I'd made it to a place where I could change out of my outerwear and then go into the pub, an hour had passed and the streets were almost completely dark. There were more people inside drinking than I had ever seen—something that would make my job that much harder. The only thing that seemed to be in my favor was the fact that the person behind the counter wasn't James, meaning that my disguise wouldn't be immediately seen through.

With a mead in my hand, I found a table to sit and watch the room. Most of the patrons were laughing, drinking, and there were a few even singing. A couple of women were circling the room, ducking over to tables to flirt with someone before either leaving or leading the man away. After awhile, I realized that the women weren't the only ones searching the place.

A familiar-looking man with gelled-back blond hair was standing against the bar. He had some form of drink in his hand that he was twirling around as he scanned the room. When we locked eyes, I remembered him as the man who had approached me the night before. A flicker of recognition appeared in his eyes and I quickly turned away. My plan had been to watch him from the corner of my eyes, but he ended up coming over and sitting across from me.

"Why, hello again."

My stomach dropped. When I spoke, I made sure that my voice was lower than usual. "Sorry, do I know you?"

"Ah, maybe not. My apologies, *sir*. You must just have one of those faces." He took a long sip of his drink but kept his eyes on me over the edge of the cup. When he put it down, he leaned across the table into my space. "So, what brings you here for the very first time?"

I bit my lip as I tried to figure out what to say. "Well, I had a lot to think about and I thought that, maybe, in a place like this, I could get a better idea as to what God's plan was. For me and for everyone else."

He nodded. "I understand. Sometimes, it can be hard to see what He wants for us."

The Unmasked Villain

"I... uh... just wish that I could hear from Him sometimes. Know His message."

The man leaned back and offered me a smile. "It sounds like you already have a good idea what it is you're looking for."

"Perhaps."

"Well then, *perhaps* I can help you." He stood up and offered me his hand. "Just follow me, *sir*."

I hesitated for a second but ended up taking his offer. The two of us walked out of the pub and began making our way down the empty back streets. As we walked, I took a small step to the side to create a slight distance between us only for the man to grab my arm with an iron grip. He turned to me with a too wide smile on his face that turned my blood cold. I returned the smile, trying to stay calm despite the obvious mistake I had made.

At some point through the walk, another man turned a corner and started jogging toward us. It was impossible to make out any details about the person from the distance, but anything had to be better than the blond man. I forced myself to trip: an action that not only forced the blond-haired man to stumble with me and, undoubtedly, catch the attention of the jogger.

I made sure my words were loud and clear when I spoke. "Please, sir, just let me go."

The man pulled me back onto my feet only to be almost immediately punched in the face. As he stumbled, the other man pulled me behind him. Now that we were closer together, I was able to see who the person was.

James stared the other man down. "Get out of here."

The blond man glanced between us before he raised his hands. "Alright. My apologies. I'll head over to the hospital on my own."

The two of us watched as the man turned and disappeared around the same corner James had come from. As soon as he was gone, James turned toward me.

"What were you thinking?"

Chapter 13

Race to the Finish

James had escorted me to the Barnes house in silence before quickly leaving, claiming that he was too angry with me to stay around. That left me to sit in the parlor on my own as the Barnes stood in the dining room, whispering to one another. It felt like I was a child again, waiting for my parents to come in and decide my punishment.

After a while, I stood up and walked into the other room. "If I may, I apologize for deceiving you and doing something dangerous. I just couldn't let this go and I figured that, like this, I could do it on my own without endangering either of you."

"But you could have been killed!" Professor Barnes shouted.

"Yes. I could have been. But I still don't regret it." When he opened his mouth, I raised my hand to show him I wasn't done. "This isn't going to stop or go away. And I understand that the two of you can't risk getting involved, but I already am. They've already been *inside* my home and hurt my family. And I will see this until the end. If that means I need to leave your home—"

"Don't be ridiculous!" Mrs. Barnes cut in. "That's not what we're upset about. We're concerned about you and your safety."

"They've been in my home and they know where you live—we're not going to be safe until they're gone!"

A silence fell over the room. After a moment, the professor cleared his throat. "Alright. What did you learn?"

"Well I'm not sure how it's related, but there was a man who seemed to know what was happening." I began explaining everything to them.

When I finished talking, Barnes stood up and moved into the parlor. A few minutes later, he came back with a map and laid it out on the table. "He said he was going to the hospital?"

Mrs. Barnes shook her head. "You can't really be trusting what he said. He obviously lied!"

"Why lie though?" I asked. "He could have just said nothing and walked away. But he didn't. He wanted me to know he to know he was going to a hospital."

"Exactly. It's not the college's—I'd like to think I would have noticed. And I think it's safe to say it's not the same one we brought Jeremy or your bother to; not only is Guy's Hospital reputable, but if it were connected to the cult, I doubt things would have ended well for any of us. Plus, it's unlikely that they'd have been able to get multiple bodies out without people noticing."

I bit my lip and tried to think about everything. It wasn't just getting people out that was a problem. From what John had said, he'd been knocked out when Jeremy had taken him to that room he'd described; that wouldn't have been easy to do without catching a few eyes.

The Unmasked Villain

"Are there any places between the pub and the market that could be considered a hospital?" I asked, leaning over the map.

The professor shook his head but before he could say anything, Mrs. Barnes let out a shaky breath. "Date Palm. It's one of the abandoned warehouses near the Thames. It's not a real hospital, but a decade ago people used to do some under the table surgeries there. It's where I got some work done. It... stopped being used after that though."

The professor reached out and placed a hand on his wife's shoulder. While a part of me wanted to ask, it was clear that it was too personal for me to dig into.

As quietly as I could, I slipped out of the room and to the kitchen. The room was small, barely big enough to hold fit the small table, chair, and stove, but each of the walls were covered in shelves. It took a while to find the tea or the kettle, but I found myself thankful for that; the more time I spent searching the place, the more time I'd give the two of them to talk.

I was in the middle of reorganizing the tea tray for a third time when Barnes walked in. "Ms. Miller, if it's alright with you, the two of us will be going to the police tomorrow morning while Elizabeth gets the house ready for your brother's arrival."

"That sounds like a good plan."

* * *

Eric's entire face had turned red. "At this point, I'm starting to think I should arrest the two of you for your own safety."

I folded my arms. "Well, if you do, I don't see how we'll be able to guide you to the cult."

"You won't be guiding us anywhere! You'll be telling us where to go and then staying here."

"If I may," the professor said as he stepped up toward the constable. "This is a very delicate operation and, as you know, we've already expressed worry about one of the officers being connected to things. If we don't say it aloud, then we can guarantee that no one will overhear and be able to warn anyone we're coming."

Eric just looked between the two of us before sighing. "I can see that Sarah's starting to make an impression on you, professor."

He laughed. "She may have given me some tips for talking with others."

"Great." Eric shook his head. "I guess I'll go get some of my officers suited and ready."

It didn't take long for the group to get ready. Seeing each man armed with a gun instead of their usual baton was strange; it seemed to alter their entire appearance. It was almost as if the guns made their bodies bigger and their eyes darker. It was chilling to see.

When we were led over to the first police carriage, I was relieved to find only the constable and Officer Conner sitting inside. While they both had guns, I knew Eric too well to be afraid of him and I knew that Conner would never risk shooting his firearm unless the situation followed the exact protocol.

The line of carriages came to a stop outside of the Endless Bottle. The officers started to pour out of them, forming a crowd in the middle of the rain. They all stared at the professor and I, waiting for a signal as to where to go without a care as to how soaked they were getting. As we walked, the people we passed stopped to watch us go to the Date Palm.

The Unmasked Villain

It didn't take long for us to make it to the building that Mrs. Barnes had pointed out to us on the map. The building was incredibly small and I wouldn't have thought it was a part of the buildings next to it if I didn't know better. A few crates had been stacked up, hiding the metal door from view.

"Is this it then?" the constable asked. When I nodded, he turned to Professor Barnes. "Please make sure that Sarah stays out here with you."

Before I could say anything, the professor let out a laugh and took me by the shoulder. Dragged over to the side, I had no choice but to watch as the officers marched into the abandoned hospital. Only half of the policemen had made it inside when the screaming started—a mixture of orders and pleas. One of the officers that hadn't made it into the building yet raised his gun into the air and fired.

I tried to take a step back but was stopped by the professor's arm. All I could do was place my hands over my ears and hope that the ringing would stop soon. Half an hour later, an officer came out with a woman in handcuffs. Soon after, more and more people were forced out. Some of them were screaming about being chosen while others just kept their heads down and walked.

Once things had calmed down. the constable came out. He looked exhausted but still smiled. "Thank you both for the help. We'll take it from here."

Barnes nodded. "When everything's all settled, would it be possible for me to speak with some of the cult members? It might help me figure out what caused those people to have rosy cheeks."

"I suppose I do owe you that much. Are you coming to the station now?"

"If we could. Then we can speak with them right after you're done with your investigation."

I cleared my throat, getting both men's attention. "Thomas is going to be discharged from the hospital soon. So, if it's alright, I think I'll sit this one out."

The professor nodded. "Then I shall see you back at the house later tonight. Let me call a carriage—"

"No, it's alright. I think I'd rather walk."

Before the two could protest, I turned and made my way down the street. With each step, I did my best to focus on the feeling of the ground under my feet and the sound of the rain hitting the street. My legs were still shaky, but I was sure that I'd be able to get the sound of the gunshot out of my head if I just kept walking.

Chapter 14

Revolutionizing Revelation

Thomas sat up in his bed, his eyes distant. His room was identical to mine, but he had no reaction to the obvious luxury that we'd never been able to afford. It hadn't been easy to get him inside the house; we'd hoped that Officer Ruggles would be able to help, but he was nowhere to be seen by the time we got back from the hospital.

The doctors had said that the drugs hadn't had any lasting effects on him—positive or negative. Unfortunately, there wasn't anything that they could do about his shoulder. Mrs. Barnes and I had been given instructions on how to keep the cuts clean and what the signs of infection were, but it was made clear that there was no way to prevent it from scarring.

I sat on the edge of the bed, holding onto a bowl of oatmeal. "I spoke with John and learned what happened. He thought that... Well, that it would help you."

Thomas turned to look at me. His words were slow and slurred, but clear. "J'hn 'ill be okay?"

"Yes. I'm sure of it. Eric will figure out what happened and everything will be back to normal before we know it."

I scooped up some of the oatmeal only to find that it had thickened to the point where it seemed practically inedible. Dropping the spoon back into the bowl, I put on the biggest smile I could. "Why don't I go get something else to eat?"

Thomas hummed but his eyes had become distant again.

When I walked into the kitchen, I found Mrs. Barnes sitting at the table, reading a pamphlet. She jumped up when she saw me. "Is he settling in alright?"

"I think so." I placed the bowl down on the table. "Are you sure that you don't want us to go back home?"

"Don't be silly. You two are more than welcome to stay as long as you need. Even after everything with this cult is made clear."

"Thank you."

"Of course. Now, what can we make that your brother will actually eat?"

"He has a sweet tooth?"

She put her hands on my shoulders and smiled. "Then let's get baking."

* * *

We were waiting for the sweetbread to finish baking when Professor Barnes came back from the station. I'd expected him to be ranting about whatever it was that he learned, but instead, he just looked exhausted. He sat down at the table and poured himself a large cup of brandy.

He took a long sip of his drink before slamming the cup against the table. "The interrogations went terrible. We could barely get anything out of them before they all started to get sick. I spent more time tending to headaches and nausea than learning what caused them to hallucinate."

"Could whatever caused them to hallucinate also be causing them to be sick?" Mrs. Barnes asked.

"Probably. But any substances could cause those symptoms if you take an improper dosage. Then there's the addition of external factors like stress, a mass psychogenic illness, or even just them all getting sick from being near one another."

I sat down at the table. "What about the man with sleeked-back blond hair? Was he there?"

"No, but the constable said that he would set up a watch at the Endless Bottle to see if he can find anyone fitting that description or anyone else from the missing persons list."

I startled at his words. In the chaos of everything that had happened, I'd completely forgotten about all of those reports. "Were all of them from that list?"

The professor nodded. "They were working on contacting the families when I left."

"Then, there are likely more victims that we haven't found yet." When Barnes raised his eyebrows, I hurried to explain myself. "There were only roughly, what, fifteen, twenty people who were taken away from the hospital? But, when I was working at the station, they were complaining about a much larger increase in missing people's cases. So, unless there is *another* event causing people to go missing..."

"Then they could be using another building as a base," the professor finished for me.

"Or at the hospital."

"I doubt it. From what the officers said, there was only one room and it could barely hold the twenty people that they found."

Mrs. Barnes frowned. "There are two or three rooms

though. One for waiting, one for operating, and... I think one for the doctors? Maybe?"

I looked between the two of them and frowned. "Then, they missed two-thirds of the place? How would that even happen?"

Barnes thought about it for a minute. "Either the cult somehow hid it or the officers purposefully ignored it. We did think that an officer was possibly involved..."

"But Eric went in with them!"

"Ms. Miller..." His voice was soft and was dripping with sympathy. It made me feel sick and as much as I wanted him to stop talking, he kept going. "Cults have a way of getting into people's heads. You've seen it for yourself. Would you have ever expected John to—"

"Stop. That's enough. Please..."

I stared at the floor, taking in the different patterns made by the wood grain. After a few deep breaths, I noticed a faint burning smell that had a hint of sweetness to it. Before I could react to it, Mrs. Barnes got up and went to the oven. She took out the buns and began busying herself with them. The professor, meanwhile, kept his focus on his drink.

I let out a sigh and both of them turned to stare at me. "If we can't trust the constable, what do we do?"

The cup made a faint thud sound as Professor Barnes placed it on the table. "I suppose that depends on what you'd like to do. It still might not be safe—"

"No, we should be fine. People saw the officers going toward Date Palm. And that one officer shot his gun. They'll need to make a statement about it. And, with so many eyes on the police and the cult, both of them would need to lay low."

The Unmasked Villain

The professor and Mrs. Barnes turned to each other. After a second, they nodded to each other and turned back to me. Barnes smiled. "Then let's think about what leads we have."

Chapter 15

Unraveling the Web

The professor and I walked up to Date Palm only to find Officer Ruggles standing outside the door. He glared at us as we got closer to the building. A part of me squirmed under his gaze, but I forced myself to appear calm. When the officer stepped up to meet us, we both smiled.

"Good morning, officer," I greeted.

"The two of you need to get out of here."

"Actually—" Professor Barnes reached into his jacket pocket and pulled out the letter that had gotten us into the second crime scene—"the constable has given us permission to investigate."

Officer Ruggles glanced over the letter for a second before sighing and handing it back to Barnes. "I'll be going in with you."

"That's fine."

We walked into the building to find a run-down room. The walls were cracked and covered in mysterious stains; while it was hard to see past the mattresses and discarded clothes, the floor didn't seem much better. A few dust-covered cupboards were set up against the far wall and filled with hand lamps and books but what caught my attention was the one that was close to the corner—the one that stood in the place Mrs. Barnes had told us there was supposed to be a door.

I glanced over at the professor who nodded at me. The two of us split up and began searching for the room. I went over to some of the discarded clothes and started mentally counting. After a few minutes had passed, I stood up, took a step forward, and pretended to fall.

When I landed, I quickly rolled over and clutched my leg. "Argh! Ow!"

In a second, the professor was next to me. "It's alright. Deep breath. Let me see it."

He lifted the skirt of my dress and then started checking my ankle. Once I felt him squeeze, I let out a small hiss. "Stop! Stop..."

"Okay. It's alright. You'll be fine." He turned toward Officer Ruggles. "I believe her ankle is broken. We need to get her to a hospital. Would you be able to go and get a carriage?"

He glanced at the both of us for a second before nodding and hurrying out of the room. We waited for a moment, making sure that he had actually left, before getting up and going to the corner of the room.

While there was plenty of dust on the cupboard, there wasn't any on the edges. The two of us had to work together, but we eventually managed to shift it to the side and reveal the door behind it.

"It was hidden," I muttered. "We only found it because of what Mrs. Barnes told us. The constable could still be..."

"Ms. Miller, I understand what you're trying to say, but we need to focus on searching this place quickly."

I nodded and tried to open the door. It required more force than I expected. When I finally managed to open it, there was a popping sound and I felt something being dragged along the floor. The operating room was completely different from how it had been described to us.

It was incredibly dark inside. I could barely make out the fact that heavy cloth covered every part of the floors and walls except for a small window that was barely visible on the left side of the room. The other thing that stood out was the shadowy mass in the center of the room. I started toward it to check whatever it was, but stopped when Barnes grabbed my shoulders.

"Ms. Miller, please return to the main room and grab one of the lamps."

I nodded and hurried back. While it was easy to find a lamp with oil inside, finding the matches we needed was much harder. I'd just managed to find some in a drawer when I heard the sound of horse hooves approaching from outside. Ruggles was back.

Running to the door we'd found, I used all my strength to move the cupboard back to where it had been before. The little bit of light that had made its way into the room was blocked, making it nearly impossible to see.

"Ms. Mill—"

"Shh!"

Before the professor could say anything else, we heard the door to the hospital opening. Two sets of footsteps echoed through the room.

A voice I didn't recognize came from the other room, their voice muffled. "No one's here, mate."

"They were a second ago..."

The footsteps grew louder and my heart dropped. I had no idea how closely Officer Ruggles was paying attention to

The Unmasked Villain

the room or how badly I'd repositioned the cupboard. I stepped back and started trying to think of an excuse.

Sneaking backward, I managed to find the professor. I threw my arm over his shoulder and leaned into his side so that he was supporting my weight. I leaned closer to where I imagined his ear would be. "Let me do the talking if they find us."

It was hard to see, but it seemed like the professor nodded.

A small scrapping sound filled the room and I braced myself to lie when the other voice I didn't recognize suddenly spoke out. "Listen, mate, they clearly already got a ride. Can I get going now?"

"Right..." As he talked, his voice became quieter. "I'm sorry about this."

"Don't be sorry, just pay me."

When the voices stopped and the door clicked shut, I let out a shaky breath. I removed my arm from Barnes and lit the lamp. Everything was bathed in an orange glow. When I turned to look in the center of the room and saw what the mass was, I almost threw up.

There wasn't any blood, but it only took one look at the body to see that it had clearly been an agonizing death. Each of the limbs was bent awkwardly and the man's face was swollen. What caught my attention was his hair. The blond strands were no longer plastered to the top of his head, but they were still clinging together.

"That's him. The man from the pub."

The two of us walked over to the man and Professor Barnes squatted down to look him over. He grabbed the man's face and started turning it side to side.

"It's hard to tell, but his cheeks aren't rosy." He lifted up the man and started pulling at his shirt. It took him a while to peel the collar over the deformed shoulder but, when he did, he frowned "He doesn't have an 'X' or a hole..."

"I don't understand." I sat down and pulled the fabric down to show his other shoulder but there wasn't anything there either. "Was he not a part of the cult?"

"Ayers didn't have the marks either. They could be the same..."

As he shifted the man's body, the professor suddenly took in a sharp breath. I turned to follow Barnes's gaze. It was hard to make out in the shadows, but there was a tiny valve in the floor. In a second, he was running around the room, running his hands along the walls like he had when he was in the pub.

After a while, he turned back around to face me, excited. "It's an air-tight room."

"And... that caused the rosy cheeks?"

"Possibly, if the room was filled with the right substances. When people drown—" I let out a shaky breath, but the professor was too caught up in his explanation to notice—"their body bloats from all the water being absorbed. Other forms of asphyxiation, meanwhile, cause your skin to take on a blue hue because of the lack of oxygen in the blood; it's all because of the lack of oxygen in their lungs.

"If they had a room like this, then that means they'd have complete control over whatever was in the person's lungs. They could fill them with whatever chemicals they wanted. They could force them to breathe methane, helium, propane, or carbon monoxide. And that lack of oxygen would also likely cause the hallucinations that made them think they were chosen by God."

"How do we figure out which gas it was?" I asked.

"I'll need to speak with the victims again; now that I know what to ask, it should be easy."

The Unmasked Villain

I bit my lip. "You want to risk the station, then?"

He shook his head. "I don't *want* to. But, there isn't anyone else we can speak with."

"There's the man at the hospital. Jeremy. We know he's been through whatever this is. I know you didn't trust his words but..."

"But we can't trust the station either." The professor sighed. "Alright. We'll go there then. We'll just have to hope Officer Ruggles left with the cabbie. Or that he has a break soon."

Chapter 16

Ticking Time Bomb

By the time we managed to slip past the officer and make our way to the hospital, the sun had started to set. The nurses made it clear visiting hours were almost over and it was only thanks to the professor's history that we were being let in at all.

We were led into the same room we'd first examined Jeremy in and found him lying on the bed. He slowly turned his head toward us. Even though he looked confused, it was easy to tell that he was at least aware of his surroundings.

When he talked, his words were slurred. "Hello."

The professor smiled and moved over to the bed. "Good evening, Jeremy. I'm Professor Zachery Barnes and this is my assistant, Ms. Sarah Miller. Do you recognize us?"

"The shops."

"Exactly. We're the ones you've met at the shops and brought you here. Do you remember what happened before that?"

"I was chosen."

The Unmasked Villain

"By God?" When Jeremy nodded, the professor continued. "When he chose you, where were you?"

"He threw me into a room. I wanted to leave. I didn't want to breathe."

I frowned. "Why not?"

"I'd never seen him so angry. It scared me."

"God?"

"The Guide."

My stomach dropped. "Who is the Guide? Do you know?"

Jeremy started shaking. "P-please. I already told the police. I already broke."

"It's alright." I placed my hand on his shoulder and offered him a small smile. "Take a deep breath. There we go. We just have a few more questions, if that's okay Jeremy."

After a while, he nodded. The professor quickly started speaking again. "When you were in the room, did you notice anything odd? Any smells or colors?"

"N-no."

"Okay. And, how long were you in the room?"

"I...I don't know. I passed out."

"How did you get away? Do you remember that?"

"I woke up. The Hand was leading me into a building. I ran. He chased after me but... you helped."

I bit my lip. He had been out of breath and exhausted when we had found him, but the idea that he could get from Date Palm to the shops without being caught didn't make sense. John had also mentioned that the two of them had been meeting at the shops rather than the Endless Bottle; I hadn't thought much about it when John first mentioned it, but now it seemed too coincidental.

"That building, was that where you were going to take John?" Jeremy nodded. "Where is it? Do you remember?"

"I do... but... please... I already broke. I told the police about the hospital. I'll be sent to hell..."

Professor Barnes stood up and started pacing the room while it took all my effort to stay standing. It had been days since the police had talked with Jeremy; they'd known the entire time.

I cleared my throat. "We just want to be sure that we have all the facts right so we can make sure everything is okay with the Guide and Hand."

It took him a second but he finally let out a shaky breath. "The old shoemaker's place."

"And the Guide? What can you say about them?"

"Black hair. Smart. I don't know... he... he doesn't show himself a lot."

"What about the Hand? What was he like?"

"He's tall. Blond. Confident."

My stomach dropped. "Does he slick his hair back?"

Jeremy nodded. "He and the Source both did."

"Source?"

"A man with lots of jewelry. Rich... I... I haven't seen him in a while."

"I see. Alright. Do you know which officer you talked to?"

Jeremy shook his head and I noticed that his whole body was shaking. There wouldn't be much else we could get out of him. Catching the professor's eyes, I shook my head to signal him to stop.

He nodded at me before offering Jeremy a smile. "Thank you for your time. We appreciate you talking with us."

As soon as we were out of the room, I turned to Barnes. "That was... insightful."

"It's probably best we wait to discuss this until after we

return home." His eyes flickered around the hallway. A few doctors and nurses were walking around. "I feel as if privacy is going to be very important for this conversation."

* * *

When our taxi pulled in behind a police carriage, I was sure I was going to be sick. The wheels had barely stopped moving before the professor threw open the door and ran inside.

"Oi! You gotta pay!"

Reaching into my bag, I pulled out a few bills. "Here. If it's not enough then you can send a bill to us at this address."

I turned and ran after the professor. By the time I reached the door, which had been left open in Barnes's haste, the yelling had started. Following the voices into the parlor, I found Professor Barnes standing in front of Mrs. Barnes, blocking her from the constable. Both men were yelling at each other; their voices were so loud it was impossible to make out what either of them was saying.

Ducking into the room, I grabbed Mrs. Barnes's hand and pulled her away from the chaos.

"Go up to Thomas's room and make sure he's okay. And whatever happens, don't let another officer inside unless he's with someone you know we can trust."

She turned and hurried up the stairs. Assured that both of them would be safe, I made my way back to the parlor. The two were still fighting; it didn't seem like either of them even noticed Mrs. Barnes leaving.

I took a deep breath before yelling as loud as I could. "Enough!"

The constable turned and glared at me. "I feel like that should be my line. What do you think you're doing, breaking into a crime scene?! Do you know how many laws that breaks? I can only cover for you both so many times!"

I stood up as straight as I could and stared him directly in the eyes. "You didn't have a problem with us going to the scene at the Thames."

"You had permission to go there! There were officers I trusted there watching over the place! And that was *before* we knew this was a cult who has been watching the two of you!"

"Before it was clear that we could 'guide' the 'hand?'"

There was a pause as the professor and I stared. The anger on Constable Fear's face shifted to confusion. "What?"

"We spoke with Jeremy."

"Mr. Graves?" He looked between us, obviously waiting for some sort of elaboration. It was easy to tell that he was genuinely confused.

All the tension drained from my body and I found myself laughing. I rushed across the room and pulled Eric into a hug.

He stiffened against me. "Ms. Miller?"

I pulled back and placed my hands on his shoulders. "We have a lot that we need to discuss."

It took us a while to explain everything to him. By the time we finished explaining everything we'd seen and figured out, his head was in his hands.

"I suppose it was foolish of me to hope that the autopsy was a clerical error."

"Do you remember who you sent to speak with Jeremy?" I asked.

"That was... Ruggles? Yes, it was, because Conner had to review the autopsy report that the professor submitted."

I grabbed at my skirt. "He was also the one who brought

The Unmasked Villain

Ayers into the interrogation room. We left the two of them alone in there."

Barnes started pacing again and his face was pale. He kept running his hands through his hair. The constable wasn't doing much better. His face was dark and he just stared off to the other side of the room.

I clapped my hands together to draw them both out of their thoughts. "Alright. Well, that's another avenue for us to explore."

Eric shook his head. "No. I need to be the one to handle that. And, once I get back to the station, I'll be doing a thorough examination of all my officers, including checking their shoulders."

"That won't guarantee anything. Not if they're the Guide." When both of the men looked at me, I just sighed. "Jeremy gave three titles: the Source, the Hand, and the Guide. From how he described them, the Source was likely Ayers and the Hand was likely the blond man who had tried to get me to go to the Date Palm. Neither of them had an 'X' on them so the Guide wouldn't either."

"I'll keep that in mind. Once we get this sorted, I'll have some officers—with *light*-colored hair—go to the shoemaker's place and look around. In the meantime, the two of you should stay here. *Please.*" When neither of us responded, he just shook his head. "We'll be there in a few hours. If we catch the both of you there, I *will* have you both arrested."

"We understand. Have a good night, Constable."

Chapter 17

Villain's Lair

The abandoned shoemaker's shop was on the edge of the street. In the past, the lights on the first and second floors had always shined through the windows as the older man who used to live there would sit and wait for customers. Those same windows were now covered by wooden planks that had started to rot from the rain.

A bell rang out when the door was pushed open. It was too dark to see anything inside; the tiny bit of light that shined in from the street only really helped to show the dust that was floating in the air. Even in the dark, it was easy to see the motion of heads turning to look up.

"Hello." My voice shook slightly.

I jumped a little when a young girl suddenly appeared in front of us; she couldn't have been older than ten years old. The dress she was wearing was not only dirty but looked worn down and on the edge of tearing. What stood out most, though, were her eyes. They were unnaturally wide and though they were slightly glazed over, something about the way she stared at the professor and I felt piercing.

The Unmasked Villain

"What are you doing here?"

"The Guide has told us to come here," I answered.

The girl stared, taking us in, before finally grunting and turning away. I relaxed for a second before noticing the other sets of eyes in the room were still trained on us. Straightening my back, I walked in with Barnes and let the door close behind us.

It took a while for me to be able to see properly in the dark and so, for a while, the only thing I could focus on was the horrible smell. The sharp scent, urine, and shit mixed with the smell of rot. When my eyes adjusted, the sight matched the scent. The shelves, tables, and counters that had once made up the shop had been replaced with mattresses lined up along the floor. While a few of the people were stumbling around, most of them were just lying there and staring. Bits of rotten, molding food were next to them along with open chamber pots, but if it bothered them, they didn't react; it was almost like they couldn't.

My stomach dropped. "They're like Thomas."

The professor placed a hand on my shoulder and started to lead me through the maze of people to the back of the room. There was a door leading to two sets of stairs—one going up and the other down. I stared at the steps leading down, unable to ignore that was where the rotting smell seemed to be coming from.

I jumped a little when Professor Barnes put a hand on my shoulder. "Let's check upstairs first."

With a nod, I hurried up the steps and through the door. The second floor only had one room; it had clearly been a bedroom at one point but was now being used as an office. The table, walls, and even parts of the floor were covered with books and papers with the only clear spots being the bed and a small path to it. Besides the bed was a box identical to the one that had been under Thomas's bed.

"Do you understand any of this?" I asked the professor as he lifted up a book.

"It seems as if they're notes on the effects of different drugs on the mind." He moved over to the bed and grabbed what looked like a notebook. He nodded to himself as he read along. "Whoever wrote this has done a lot of experiments."

"What do you think they were trying to do?"

He flipped through another few pages. "I think... they were looking for ways to help someone with brain damage."

"Well, that's... that's a good thing. Right?"

He put the book back down and turned to me. "If this data hasn't been altered in any way. And, assuming, of course, that the man behind the journal didn't also cause the brain damage."

I wrapped my arms around myself and let out a shaky breath. "You think that was the point in giving them the gas?"

"It's possible."

I shook my head, trying to calm down. "I... I think that I'll go take another look around the first floor. See if any of the people down there can give us some more information about the Guide."

Before Barnes could respond, I hurried back down to the first floor. A few of the people turned to look at me but most of them kept their gaze toward the front door.

I scanned the crowd and found the young girl from the door staring at me from one of the beds. When I sat down beside her, she shifted to lean against me with a small whimper.

"Are you okay?" I asked.

The Unmasked Villain

"Headache's back."

I ran my hand through her hair. It was incredibly knotted and she whimpered slightly as my fingers got caught. After a while, I started to hum. As I did, the girl's body started to relax.

When she finally seemed calm, I cleared my throat. "Were you also chosen?"

"Yeah. I was."

My chest started to ache and I closed my eyes. "Do you remember anything about the person who told you that you were chosen?"

"They kept calling him the Hand. He was friends with the Source. I didn't like him. He seemed mean—the Source, that is. The Hand was kinda cool. Gave me lottsa food."

"I see... Can you tell me more about them? Or the Guide?"

"The Hand stayed with the Source a lot. I don't know much 'bout the Guide. He just brings people upstairs or downstairs. I saw it once, ya know. Do you wanna see?"

Before I could answer, the girl forced herself up and started toward the door. With no choice, I followed after her. She was breathing heavily but the smell, which got worse as we went further down, didn't seem to bother her. When she opened the door, I suddenly understood why the smell hadn't bothered me before. I almost vomited as the smell hit me.

It was then that I noticed the shapes on the other side of the room. A number of tables had been set up along the walls, countless hooks had been hung from the ceiling, and everywhere I looked there were dead bodies. The ones on the tables had had their heads and chests cut open while the ones on the hooks seemed to be having their blood drained into bowls below them.

"When we go to Him," the girl said, "the Guide takes us down here so we can keep helping."

I grabbed the girl's arm and pulled her behind me. Even with the door slammed shut, I could still see the bodies.

Scooping the girl up into my arms, I ran up the stairs.

"Professor! Professor!"

In a second, Professor Barnes was running down to us. "What is it? Is everything okay?"

"The basement. It's—" My body retched at the thought of what I'd seen.

Before I could say anything else, the professor stepped around the two of us and walked down the stairs. Even from the landing, I could see the bodies. Each one of them was staring at me. Their eyes were bright and full of hatred.

"Did you think you could help?"

I looked around, trying desperately to find the source of the voice. It was familiar but I couldn't quite place my finger on it; something about it felt too hateful. I was sure that whoever it was would never talk to me like that—even though I deserved it.

A hand landed on my shoulder and I jumped. The professor was in front of me, but I couldn't remember him walking up to me. When two of his fingers landed against my neck, I realized just how fast my heart was pounding.

"Are you experiencing visions?"

"I... the bodies... talked..."

"Carbon monoxide."

"W-what?"

Professor Barnes grabbed me and the young girl and started to pull us out to the main room on the first floor. "Everyone, get outside! Now!"

A few of the people struggled to get up and followed after us as Barnes forced us to the door. The rain had started to come down hard while we were inside and soon I found myself drenched. But, even though I was soaked and freezing, I found that I didn't care: breathing had become far easier.

I turned and found the professor rushing back toward the door, helping people as they stumbled out. When I stepped toward him, he held up his hand. "Stay here. Focus on breathing."

While a part of me wanted to argue, I found myself just sinking to the ground instead. I just breathed. In. And out.

Chapter 18

Dangerous Showdown

I was still feeling a little nauseous when the young girl came and sat down next to me. She'd been one of the first ones that the professor had checked on after everyone had gotten out of the shop. Her age and size had apparently made her more at risk than some of the others, but, thankfully, she'd been mostly okay.

After a moment of hesitation, she leaned against my side. "I'm sorry if the basement scared ya."

"It's alright, dear. That wasn't your fault." I bit my lip, trying to think of the best way to ask my next question. "You mentioned that the Guide was the one who brought people down there. Can you tell me more about that?"

"Not really. Sometimes, when people got really sick, he'd take 'em upstairs. Then, sometime later, he'd drag 'em down. Hand usually had to help with it when he dropped off new chosen—said the Guide wasn't strong enough to move people on his own."

"And.." I licked my lips. "What did he look like? Guide?"

"I didn't see him often. Uh, he had black hair? I don't really know what else. It was hard to see."

The Unmasked Villain

"That's okay. That was really helpful." I looked up at the sky, letting the rain smack against my face. It was hard to tell from all the clouds, but it seemed like a few hours had already passed. The police would be here soon. "What's your name, sweetie?"

"Abbie."

"Well, Abbie, I'm afraid that me and my friend are going to have to leave soon. And, after we do, the police will come by—" She stiffened against me and I threw my arm around her in a small hug... "One of them is the constable. You can call him Constable Eric. When he shows up, can you tell him what you told me?"

"I'm not sure..."

"It'll be alright. He's a big softie. Just give him the biggest, saddest eyes that you can and he'll let you do whatever you want."

"And if he doesn't?"

"Then that's when you give him a bit of lip and do what you want anyways."

That was enough to make her giggle. With a final squeeze, I stood up and made my way over to Professor Barnes who was checking the eyes of a man. When he saw me approaching, he nodded.

With a final few words to the man, he turned and jogged over to me. "I know. We need to go."

He grabbed my arm and the two of us made our way through the crowd. As we approached the more active part of the street, it was easy to hear the sound of hooves against the cobblestone.

They'll take care of them, I told myself.

"They will. And I'll be sure to write a letter to whatever hospital they are sent to with my suggested course of action to help them recover. It won't help with the brain damage, but at least the other symptoms will be managed."

"Is that it then? We found the cause?"

"Yes. Carbon monoxide would match all the symptoms. And, it's quite possible that it can make the face take on a rosy appearance in death."

"So..." It was hard to choke out the next few words, "we're done then?"

"It would seem so. The police will be able to take over the rest."

I unlinked my arm from the professor's. "I need some time alone. To think."

"Of course, Ms. Miller. Take your time."

Without looking back, I made my way down the street.

* * *

Even with a crime scene a few streets away, the Endless Bottle was incredibly crowded. I walked up to the counter, hoping to find James, only to see one of his coworkers instead. While the man was kind enough, I found myself unable to discuss my real struggles with him leaving me with only the mead for comfort.

By the time I'd reached the end of the fifth cup, I'd made up my mind. Between the mysterious individual who had reported the first body, the window in the cloth room, and the drugs that had been under Thomas's bed appearing at the shoe shop, there were too many threads left for me to let it go. Even if the professor decided he was done, I couldn't stop.

Paying my tab, I stumbled out of the pub. A part of me wanted to go to the Date Palm right away, but I knew better. There would be no way that I could investigate when I could barely stay on my feet. Cursing myself for going too far, I hailed a carriage and sat in a pleasant silence back to the Barnes's home.

When the taxi pulled to a stop a few blocks away, I frowned. "Not there yet."

"Sorry, ma'am. There's too many police carriages for me to get closer."

My stomach dropped and in a second I sobered up. Taking out the money from my purse, I handed it to the man and jumped out. The rain was cold as it pelted my face and soaked my dress. I must have looked mad by the time I reached the first line of officers.

"Sorry, ma'am. This area is off-limits."

I glared at the man. I didn't recognize him from around the station and, judging from his uniform, he was a street bobby; if he spent his time patrolling the streets, he likely didn't recognize me either. I had no chance of reasoning with him. "Is the constable here?"

"That's none of your—"

"Eric!" I yelled, cutting the man off. "Eric! Professor! Mrs. Barnes!"

"Ma'am, please, you're causing a disturbance."

"Eric! Professor!"

The street bobby reached out and grabbed my shoulder. "Ma'am, if you don't leave, I will have to detain you."

From behind the bobby, someone cleared their throat. When I looked over the man's shoulder, I felt my hopes crumble. Instead of one of the people I'd called for, Officer Conner was standing there.

"Allow me to handle this, Fox." The street bobby stiffened and, with a quick nod, walked away. With no one else around, Conner turned to me with a glare. "Ms. Miller."

I bit my lip, trying to think of anything I could say. In

the end, there was nothing. "I'm sorry about before. Just, please, tell me if Mrs. Barnes and Thomas are okay."

He stared at me for what felt like an eternity before sighing. "By all accounts, Officer Miller is present at the scene."

"I know he's here, but is he okay?"

He rolled his eyes. "He's fine. And, due to his presence, if *Officer Miller* were to be on the scene and spoke with some of the people on the scene, I'm sure that that would make full sense in the report."

My heart jumped. "Really?"

"Just don't actually try and investigate anything."

"Thank you, Conner!"

Before he could change his mind, I ran past the officers and into the house. The usually clean rooms had been completely destroyed. Books from the shelves had been knocked over and some of the furniture had been tipped or knocked down. It was clear that whatever happened, hadn't been peaceful. From upstairs, I could hear voices. Without missing a beat, I ran toward them.

Nothing had been touched in Thomas's room. The book I'd been reading to him was still on the side table along with a plate of half-eaten cookies and the curtains were still drawn open—even now with the lamps light. The only real difference was that Thomas was no longer lying in bed by himself. A few officers were standing around him as he sat up in the bed, crying.

In a second, I was across the room and pulling him into my arms. "You're okay. Thank God, you're okay."

He hummed slightly, but didn't speak. A second later, I found myself supporting his whole weight.

One of the officers cleared their throat. "You must be

Sarah, Thomas's sister. He talked about you a lot before... well..."

I nodded and offered the man a smile, trying my best to seem as if I knew whoever this man was. "Yes. I am. Is he okay? Do you... do you know what happened here?"

"He's fine. The attacker only seemed to be targeting the... uh..." He hesitated for a moment, trying to find the right words, "the other person in the house."

"The professor? Or Mrs. Barnes?" When he didn't respond to my question, I turned to my brother. "Thomas, who else was here at the time? Can you tell me?"

"M'ss."

I nodded. "And, do you know what happened to her?"

"Gone... 'elp." As he spoke, his eyes started to shine and his body began shaking. "Couldn't... go fast 'nough."

"That's okay. You did your best. Is there anything else you remember happening?"

"Screamin.'"

With a final hug, I turned to the officers in the room. Each of them was looking away, but it was clear they'd been watching us. "Do you know where Professor Barnes is?"

"No clue. Sorry."

"And Mrs. Barnes? Do you know where she's been taken for help?"

"College hospital. Constable Fear was really clear about that."

I nodded and turned to Thomas. "I'll be back as soon as I've checked on her, alright? Just focus on staying safe until then."

With a quick kiss to his forehead, I turned and walked out of the room. It didn't take long for me to find Officer Conner downstairs. While the other officers were running around, he stood in the parlor just staring at the scene in front of him. Blood was splattered on the ground and over some of the furniture. I focused on the table. Three tea cups had been set up and steam was still coming out from each of the cups.

"Do I need to tell you that there were two attackers?" I asked.

"Offi—" Conner cut himself off and shook his head. "Ruggles claims he was the only one. And the blood splatter matches with a hit from one of our batons."

"But the tea—"

"Is speculation. We need to follow protocol, Ms. Miller."

"And if you didn't need to?"

He let out a sigh. "Is there something I can help you with?"

"Does the professor know about this?"

"The constable sent some people to look for him. He's probably at the hospital."

"I see. Then, who discovered the scene?"

"...You don't already know?" When all I did was smile, he glared at me. "James Bullard. He was apparently coming to visit your brother. He saw Mrs. Barnes bleeding and ran to get help."

I frowned. "He did?"

Conners hummed. "Probably still at the hospital if you want to question him."

"But... he just went and reported it?"

"Do you think everyone who reports a crime is a criminal?"

"No... I just..." I shook my head. "Thank you, Conner. I'll go check on Mrs. Barnes now."

As I was leaving the room, I heard Conner clear his throat. "Be careful."

"You too, officer."

Chapter 19

Final Heart-Stopping Revelation

From the police officers standing outside, it was easy to tell which room I was looking for. Thankfully, they recognized me and let me inside without much fuss. When I got inside, though, I almost wished they had turned me away.

Mrs. Barnes's face was almost unrecognizable. Not only had it already started to turn purple and black, but a large portion of it had become swollen or scabbed over. If it weren't for the professor sitting beside the bed, holding her hand, I might not even be able to tell it was her. Her chest was covered in a bandage and, even though they were clearly fresh, blood was already starting to seep to form an "X."

While the couple didn't react to me, Constable Fear walked over to me from the other side of the room. He placed a hand on my shoulder and led me out of the room and down the hall.

Before he could say anything, I cut in. "Is she going to be okay?"

"They're not sure right now. The doctors say it's... very bad."

I let out a shaky breath. "What happened with Ruggles?"

"He apparently was let into the house and then, when she had her back turned, he attacked her for... pretending to be a woman."

"You know that's a lie, right? Mrs. Barnes had *no* reason to allow him inside. She knew that there were members of the cult in the police. She was there when we talked about Ruggle's part of it!"

"I know."

"Then you know the rest of it is also a lie. At the very least, there were *two* people at the scene."

"Ms. Miller... Sarah. I understand that you want to figure out what happened, but we both know that this was *because* the two of you were investigating."

I stepped back. "I know. But, after all of this, I can't turn away."

He ran a hand down his face before sighing. He reached into his pocket and pulled out a money clip. Shoving some money into my hands, he stared me in the eyes. "This is for a ride back to the hospital. If you are not here by this time tomorrow, I will be sending out every officer to every part of the city to find you."

"Thank you, Eric."

"Don't thank me. Just... be safe."

I nodded. "I will be. Now, if you excuse me, I have someone to interrogate."

Before the constable could say anything to me, I turned and hurried down the hall.

* * *

The Unmasked Villain

With the holding cells were filled with people, it was easy to find Ruggles. The man had been put into his very own cell and was leaning against the bars. As I walked up to him, he and every other person in the area turned to watch my every step.

As I stood in front of him, I tried to ignore everyone else and just think about how to best talk to him. He'd always seemed professional, but I doubted it would be anything like talking to Conner.

"Hello again, Officer Ruggles. I was hoping that we could have a bit of a chat."

"I already made what happened clear."

"You broke into a woman's home and attacked her because you didn't agree with how she lived her life?"

"That's what I said."

"Actually, you said you were invited in. So, now that we've cleared that part up, why don't you tell me what *actually* happened." When he turned away from me, I shifted to the side so that I could see a part of his face. "Was Mr. Ayers also 'pretending' to be something? Is that why you killed him?"

"I didn't."

"Oh, no? And, I guess you didn't carve that 'X' into the door either. Though, it wasn't there when Mrs. Barnes and I left, and whoever did it clearly spent a long time on it. If you showed up right away, how did you miss the person?"

He stepped away from the bars and deeper into the cell. I was making him uncomfortable. "You can ignore me, but the constable already knows you're involved in all of this. He knows about the autopsy report and the interview with Jeremy.

"Though, I guess you don't care if you're caught. It's

your partner you want to cover up. The one you and Mrs. Barnes had tea with before you attacked her."

He stiffened. "I was alone."

"No. You weren't alone." I thought about the three people that Jeremy had described: the Guide, the Source, and the Hand. If the Hand was the blond-haired man then that left the Source and the Guide. Ayers had worn a lot of jewelry which would have made him the Source. "You were with the Guide."

Ruggles turned around and stomped up to the bars. "Let's say you're right about all of this. That I am a part of the chosen. Why would I have killed the Source?"

"I don't know..." I smiled. "But how would you have known that Ayers was the Source otherwise?"

A hand shot out from between the bars and pulled me forward. A second before I smacked into the bar, another hand appeared from the side to cushion the impact. I turned and found John reaching his arm out of the cell toward me. His hand fell past my head to grab Ruggles's arm.

"Let her go."

As soon as I was free, I stepped closer to John's cell. "Thank you."

John nodded at me before turning toward Ruggles. "I may not know as much as you do about all of this, but I'm fairly certain He would never tell us to attack anyone."

"A fake like you has no right to tell me what He would want."

"Are you sure you're not the fake? Killing one of the leaders—that sounds a lot like someone who wasn't really chosen."

"No! No! The Hand should never have marked you. They only accepted you to hurt the Guide—the real connection to God."

The Unmasked Villain

John frowned. "Why would me being chosen hurt the Guide?"

Ruggles went pale and turned away but it was already too late. I thought about everything that had happened; the same drugs from the shoemaker's shop had been under Thomas's bed and the blond man who kept approaching me had been beaten to death and hidden away. My stomach twisted. I shook my head to push those thoughts and suspicions away.

Taking a deep breath, I turned toward John. "Do you remember if you saw anyone besides Jeremy approach you about the group? Or anything else about the situation?"

"No. I... I said everything I knew in the interrogation."

I turned to look at all the other people in the cells. I recognized some of them as the healthier ones from the shoemaker's shop and a few others from Date Palm. Each one of them looked exhausted.

Clearing my throat, I moved into the center of the hall. "Excuse me. Is anyone here willing to tell me more about being Chosen?"

My eyes scanned the room only to find that, suddenly, no one wanted to look at me. Letting out a shaky breath, I tried again. "I know that it's hard to face, but the Guide hurt you. Some of you in ways that will follow you for the rest of your life. The officers and I want to make sure that he atones for it."

Before I could try something else, John stepped to the edge of his cell. "Did anyone else get that message just now? He spoke to me. He wants us to help this woman."

After a few seconds, more and more people started to walk up to the door of their cells and speak out. I shot John a quick smile before going around and listening to what each person had to say. Their stories were all the same: a blond man, who they'd come to know as the Hand, would approach them and show them that He was looking to contact them. They'd go to the Date Palm, enter the cloth room, and "convene" with God. From there, they'd be given the option to become Chosen or to leave His words behind. After, they'd get branded by the Source's ring—a permanent symbol that would always allow them access to the room in Date Palm where they could speak with God. Occasionally, they'd see and speak with the Guide so that he could record and decode what He had said.

"Does anyone know how many other Chosen there are?"

Everyone started responding all at once. Some people were claiming that this was all there was while others insisted that there were thousands. When someone tugged on my skirt, I turned. Curled up in the corner of one of the cells was Abbie.

I squatted down and smiled at her. "Hello again. How are you doing?"

"It's loud."

The debate as to how many Chosen there kept going around us. "It is, isn't it? I think that's my fault. I thought there might be a more solid answer."

She shrugged. "They're all right."

"What do you mean?"

"There are lottsa Chosen, but mostta them are dead."

I took a deep breath. "How... do you know that?"

"I saw the Hand throwing 'em into the Thames. That's partta why he picked me up."

The image of the horrifying basement jumped into my mind alongside the two other bodies that had been laid out. The thought that there were more victims hidden in the muck made my chest feel cold.

"Thank you for telling me, Abbie." Standing, I turned to

The Unmasked Villain

John. "Would you be able to go around and see if anyone remembers specific names?"

"Okay. What about you?"

"Well, it seems like everyone's all been to the hospital. Maybe if I go there, I can find something else out." I turned and walked down the hall, doing my best to remain calm.

Chapter 20

Unmasked Truth

The Date Palm didn't have any officers stationed outside of it this time. It made sense, in a way: most of the officers would either be getting checked for an "X" or at the shoemaker's shop.

Walking into the secret room, I was thankful to find that the body of the blond man—the Hand— had been removed. All that was inside now was the cloth that had been set up along the walls. I approached the window. Up close, I could just faintly make out some scratch marks; it looked as if someone had tried to escape but had only managed to weaken the window slightly.

I raised the spare lamp I had grabbed from the waiting room and started to smash it against the glass. It ended up taking more tries than I would have liked, and by the time I'd gotten it to smash my arms felt numb, but it had worked. Kicking out a few of the loose shards from the sill, I hoisted myself up into the other room.

It was clear that somebody had been living inside. Old bits of food were scattered around on the table mixed with notes. It was hard to understand what they said. Most of the words were ones that I didn't recognize or what seemed to be some kind of shorthand. But, even without understanding it, I could recognize the handwriting.

Grabbing a few of the papers, I crawled back out the window and started to make my way toward the Endless Bottle. When that person wasn't there, I left and went to his apartment.

After a few knocks, James opened the door. The smile he offered me quickly fell away and he ushered me inside to the couch.

"What's wrong?"

I unfolded the papers and held them out so he could see. As soon as he recognized them, his face went pale. He tried to grab them out of my hand, but I pulled them away before he could. "How could you do this?"

"Ms. Miller, please. I'm trying to do the right thing. I swear it."

"You swear it? To who? God? Who *chose* you?"

His expression shifted. "You weren't this mad at John when you found out he was a part of this."

"Don't treat it like it's the same thing. John wasn't at the start of this whole thing! But this—" I pointed at the papers in my hands—"tells me that *you* were."

His eyes scanned the papers. "You don't even know what those say. If you did then... then you'd see that I'm just trying to help."

"Help who? Thomas?" When his eyes widened, I let out a small, bitter, laugh, "I'm not an idiot. And I don't need to read this to know that the drugs at that damned store are the same as the ones from under his bed.

"And I also don't need to talk to him to know that *this* isn't what he would want—before or after the accident. He cared about people. He was a police officer for God's sake!"

"And he will be again. I just... need more time."

I bit my lip, my anger fading away slightly. "Then, you don't regret any of it?"

"Of course, I regret parts of it!" He ran his hand through his hair. "I tried to keep you and John out of it, I really did! Members were told to not recruit others and Vincent was told to stay away. But he just wouldn't leave you alone after we had to cut Ayers. Every time I turned around, he seemed to be with you at the bar—tried to take you to the hospital! If everything had just worked the way it was supposed to then..."

I stood up and started to make my way toward the door. When a hand landed on my shoulder, I tried to shrug it off but he only tightened his hold and spun me around. His eyes were sharp as he glared right at me.

"What else was I supposed to do? Nothing?"

"That's better than becoming—" I couldn't force the word out of my mouth, "Becoming *this*."

"But becoming *this* will let me pay Mr. Miller back!" When I shook my head, he let out a mad laugh. "I thought you wanted us to do what we needed to be happy no matter what others think?"

My stomach dropped. "You can't really be trying to say—"

"I'm just saying that my goal is to make everyone happier. Please, Ms. Miller. If you won't let this go for me, do it for your brother—do it for John." I grabbed his arms by the wrist and forced them off of me. When I started to walk away, he reached for me again. "Leave the papers."

I considered it for a second before pushing the papers into his chest.

"Thank you," he said.

I tried to walk away, but he just tightened his grip again.

The Unmasked Villain

"Let go of me."

"You wouldn't tell the constable... would you?"

When I didn't respond right away, he started to pull me deeper into the apartment. I tried to take my arm back, but he wouldn't let go. His nails were digging into my arm and my hand was starting to feel numb. No matter how much I struggled, he wouldn't let me go. He pulled me toward a door and tossed me inside.

I spun around and kicked. While it was enough to make James flinch, it wasn't enough to give me enough space to get by. He grabbed me when I tried to slip by and forced me down onto the floor. My head smacked against the floor and for a second, I couldn't see anything.

When I finally managed to get some vision back I could make out the blurry image of James standing over me with something in his hands. I tried to swat him away, but my arm hit nothing. There was nothing I could do and soon I felt a prick on my arm.

"I really am sorry, Ms. Miller."

It didn't take long for exhaustion to take over. I tried to keep my eyes open, but between the dull pain from the back of my head and the drugs, there was no way I could fight it. The last thing I felt before I fell asleep was James lifting me up by my shoulders and starting to drag me somewhere.

* * *

The first thing that I noticed when I woke up was that slight jostling of my seat. When I noticed the sound of hooves, it became clear that I was in a carriage. Opening my eyes slightly, I found that James was sitting next to me. His hair had been pushed back and his face was even paler than normal. A part of me wanted to reach out and offer help but the pounding headache was enough of a reminder of what happened and kept me from doing so.

He turned to me and caught my eyes before I could close them. I watched as he reached into his pocket and pulled out a syringe.

"There's no point in that." It took all my energy to force the words out of my mouth and even then they came out as a slurred mess. Still, based on how he hesitated, he must have understood me.

"I just need some time to think. I can fix things if I just..."

I watched as he put his head in his hands. Getting angry hadn't helped—he'd just gotten defensive. Taking a risk, I put my hand on his back and started to rub small circles into it. He started to relax under me.

I swallowed hard. "You haven't seen Thomas since the hospital, right?"

"I... I haven't."

"He's doing a lot better. They think the drugs are helping him."

James looked up at me. "Really?"

"Would you... like to see him? He's still at the Barnes house." I felt his back stiffen and quickly guessed where I'd faltered. "They don't know about you. I figured that out on my own. They should just let us in."

"And after?" His voice was cold.

I licked my lips. "You can speak with the professor, if you'd like. He did promise to help you and John get into the college, you know."

He laughed, "I don't think he or his wife will be happy to speak with me."

"Then, we move. The four of us. We can just get away from all of this."

"I thought you wanted to send me to the constable."

"I... I was upset at first, but you're right. You did what you could to be happy—to make our family happy. Even if I don't like how you did it... I'll always support you."

He pulled me into a hug. "Thank you."

"O-of course. I'm..." It was hard to force the words out, but I knew I needed to. "I'm proud of you. Always have been, always will be."

James pulled back and smiled at me. Before I could offer to tell the driver the address, he knocked on the window and gave it himself. When he turned back and beamed at me, I did my best to match it while thinking about how he knew where the couple lived.

After a while, I cleared my throat. "What are the meanings behind those names anyways? Source? Guide? They don't seem like the kind of things you would pick."

"I didn't pick them—Ayers did. He called himself the Source because he was the funds and the start of it all. Vincent was the Hand because he did most of the physical work, and I was the Guide because I was the one guiding the research."

"It must have been hard, cutting off the other two." I watched James for any shift in body language. While his expression darkened, his body remained relaxed.

"They were going to do it to me. I'm not the first Guide, apparently. Ayers got drunk and admitted as much. They just... took out the last one because he wasn't following orders well enough. So, I set Ayers up to take the fall. Set up some of the bodies and then reported them." He turned to me and I tried my best to not show any sort of reaction to his admission that he'd been the one to report Ms. Donna's body. "I didn't mean for him to get killed, though. That was just... a last resort that Ruggles was only meant to take if he needed to."

"Well, I'm glad you're okay."

I pulled him into a small hug and looked out the window. We were almost to the Barnes's home and, to what I could only still hope, a swarm of officers.

Chapter 21

Resilience and Redemption

My eyes darted around as soon as we were out of the carriage. While a few of the officers watched us, none of them moved to stop us from entering the house like they had when I was there earlier. Every time I tried to catch one of the officer's eyes, they just nodded and went about whatever it was they were doing beforehand.

I looked into the parlor as we passed only to find it empty. Mentally cursing, I hurried up the steps and to Thomas's room. Seeing Officer Conner standing next to the bed beside Thomas, I could barely hold back a relieved laugh.

"Officer." I greeted. "I hope you don't mind I brought along James. He's a family friend."

He nodded. "I remember. He's the man who reported the attack."

"He's had a bit of bad luck with things like this lately." I looked Conner right in the eyes. "Apparently, he's the one who reported poor Ms. Donna."

I hurried over to the writing desk and brought the chair

over. When James sat down, I judged the distance between him and Thomas. Even if he tried something, there would be enough space for Conner or I to jump between them. Satisfied, I patted the seat.

As James sat down, Thomas looked up at me. His eyes were distant but his eyebrows were drawn together. Stepping around the chair, I placed a quick kiss to his forehead and shifted to whisper in his ear. "Trust me."

Thomas grunted and slowly turned away from me. When James reached out and placed a hand on Thomas's knee, I barely managed to stop myself from pushing him off. Instead, I turned away and walked to stand next to Officer Conner.

As I was looking for the right words, Conner smirked at me. "I suppose you've changed your mind about the person who reported the body?"

"No. I haven't." I swallowed hard. "In fact, I'd say that I'm more sure of it than ever."

After a moment, he nodded. "Alright. Well, protocol states—"

"Please, Conner. Just..." I tried to think of what to say to prevent James from understanding it. " I have an appointment with a friend at the hospital. Would you be able to send someone to tell him that I can't make it?"

After a second, he nodded and walked out of the room. I turned back to watch as James and Thomas talked. From a glance, it was clear just how uncomfortable the whole thing was making Thomas and I couldn't help but wonder how long that had been going on. How had I not noticed when James had come to visit before?

I moved to stand beside my brother. "What are the two of you talking about?"

"I'm just checking his mental state. He seems to be

regressing slightly—more closed off and not talking." James glanced at me from the corner of his eye. "You said that the drugs were helping him?"

"He must just be tired. It's been a long day and I'm sure the police have been questioning him quite a bit."

"That's true. We should probably leave him to rest."

I mentally cursed at myself. "I'm sure we can stay a bit longer. He's missed you, isn't that right, Thomas?"

He grunted.

"Ms. Miller... Is there a reason you want us to stay?"

My stomach dropped and I couldn't figure out how to respond. James stood up. Before he could move, I jumped on him. My weight was enough to force him to fall over. The chair landed on the floor first and ended up breaking under us. James's head bounced off the floor and his eyes closed as he tried to curl in on himself around me.

There was no way that I'd be able to keep him down and I wasn't sure how fast any of the officers in the house could react. I reached into his jacket and went for where I knew there would be a pocket. The glass of the syringe was cold and felt heavy in my hand.

When I sat up, I looked for any bit of exposed flesh that I could stab the needle. The only option I had was the neck. My hand was shaking as I stabbed it in. My hand hovered over the plunger but I found myself hesitating; I had no idea what was in the needle, how much was in the needle, or even if I was using it right.

Before I could steel myself, I found myself falling to the floor with a dull ache on my nose. By the time I managed to collect myself, James was already standing up and tossing the needle to the floor. I stood up only to have a hand wrap around my neck and force me back against the wall.

His eyes were wide and his breathing was frantic. "You lied."

"James, please—"

"You. LIED."

My eyes darted to the door but no one appeared. With no other choice, I reached up and grabbed the hand around my throat. He wasn't squeezing or pushing down on it, but that didn't stop the threat of it.

"Let's take a deep breath, James. I think we've both over-reacted—"

"You want to hand me over."

"No. Ja—" I cut myself off when I felt the pressure on my throat. I tried to pull the hand off, but his grip tightened. "James."

"I'm just trying to make us happier. I'm doing this for our family."

I couldn't respond—I couldn't do anything but try and breathe. I was so out of it, that I didn't notice the needle getting stabbed into James's neck or even the hand dropping me. What finally brought me back was the sound of crying.

James was lying on the floor with one hand raised up to where the needle had been stabbed. Beside him, Thomas was sat down, tears falling down his face. When I slipped down the wall, he turned and started crawling toward me. His movements were still shaky and it was only me reaching out and grabbing him that prevented Thomas from falling over.

For a while, the two of us just sat there, hugging each other. Even when the door to the room opened and Officer Conner walked in, Thomas stayed curled up next to me. There was nothing I could do but hold my brother as a few of the officers came in and carried James away.

After a while, Conner cleared his throat. "The constable

should be here in about twenty minutes. Typically, I would be the one to take your statement but... if you'd prefer to wait..."

"Thank you."

He nodded before shifting to lean against the wall. I blinked and he was gone. Before I could figure out where he went, I blinked again and the constable was sitting on the ground in front of me. He had a hand on my shoulder and the other on Thomas's.

"Eric?"

"It's okay. It's over. We're going to get the two of you to the hospital, alright?"

I felt myself being lifted up and led away. The entire trip, I felt floaty. Only Thomas's hand in mind and the constable's hand on my shoulder kept me grounded. Letting out a shaky breath, I looked up. "What will happen now?"

"It depends. From what we've learned, most of the members of the cult haven't actually committed a crime, though, they might have to be taken to an institute."

"Including John? And... James?"

The constable looked between the two of us. "Let's discuss this more later. For now, just relax."

I nodded. As badly as I wanted to know, I didn't have the energy to make it through the conversation. Instead of fighting, I closed my eyes and leaned back in the seat. My adrenalin had completely faded away, leaving me with nothing. By the time we pulled up to the hospital, I was more than happy to have a nurse help me inside.

The check-up didn't take long. They quickly determined that there wasn't any damage to my trachea and that there weren't any other issues. There was more care given to Thomas's examination—the nurses wanted to be sure that he understood all of their questions but wouldn't let me inside to help them. With nothing else to distract myself with, I had no choice but to face the Barnes.

I sat down next to the professor and he turned to look me over. When he noticed my throat, he reached out and pulled me into a hug. "I'm sorry."

"What do you have to apologize for? If anything, it should be me. I... I didn't notice him acting differently. I didn't stop him... I..." A sob broke through me and I found myself unable to stop. Barnes handed me a handkerchief and I used it to muffle the sounds. When I gathered myself enough, I turned to look at Mrs. Barnes. My voice was small and scratchy. "Will she be okay?"

The professor grabbed Mrs. Barnes's hand and brought it to his lips. "She's been through a lot. This won't be the thing that beats her."

I took a shaky breath and stood up. With a final nod, I turned and walked out of the room. In terms of goodbye, I knew it was terrible but it was also all that I could handle.

THE END

Epilogue: New Horizons

The pea soup had long become cold on the bedside table as I read *Frankenstein* out loud. It was hard to get through the text, but it was clear that Thomas was enjoying it. We had just gotten to the monster's point of view when there was a knock at the front door. I frowned and put the book down on the bed.

"That'll be Eric."

Thomas hummed and offered me a small, lopsided smile; it was an action that he'd been doing a lot over the few weeks since the case had been closed. Each time I saw him like that, I wanted to break down in tears.

It would never be the same, but at least he was here.

I turned and hurried down the stairs and toward the incessant knocking.

When I opened the door, I was surprised to find Professor Barnes standing there with a large basket in one hand filled to the brim with buns. "Ms. Miller."

"Professor! I wasn't expecting you. Come in."

Turning, I led the professor down the hall and to the parlor where I'd set up a tray with tea and sweets. Seeing them, the professor turned to me. "Were you expecting company?"

"Just the constable. He's coming by to discuss Thomas's job and my time as Officer Miller. But feel free to have some."

"No, no, that's alright. I shouldn't stay long." He turned and handed me the basket. "Here. These are just a gift from Elizabeth."

I felt my shoulders relax. "She's okay then?"

"Still on bed rest, though that didn't stop her from following me to the kitchen and ordering me to make these."

"I'm glad to hear it." I sat down on one of the sofas and gestured for him to follow. "Is there something you needed?"

"Just checking in on you and Thomas. We haven't heard from you since... well... everything."

"We're doing well, thank you."

"That's wonderful. And... what about John?"

"Thomas told the judge that he didn't want there to be any punishment, but due to his condition, it didn't end up counting for much. He did get a lesser sentence, though. Three years of imprisonment." A silence fell over us and I knew what he was trying to avoid asking. "James... won't be getting the same treatment."

"I'm sorry. That must be hard on you."

I shook my head. "He murdered and hurt so many people. I... I knew that the death penalty was the only option."

"Still this has to be hard. Elizabeth and I are here for you."

"Thank you. I appreciate it."

The professor turned and began to pace a few steps along the length of the table before clearing his throat. "Will you be taking a position at the station then?"

The Unmasked Villain

I laughed. "I doubt that's what the constable has in mind."

"But... if he does offer you a job?"

"I hadn't really thought about it, if I'm honest." I frowned to myself. "I'm... glad that we were able to get to the bottom of this whole incident, even with how it ended. But, at the same time, I think that if I had to go through that all again I'd end up losing my mind."

The professor let out a small laugh and put his hand on my shoulder. "Well, I think that this was a bit of a special case. But, I'm glad to hear that you won't be resigning any time soon."

"Resigning? From what?"

The professor took his hand away. "As my assistant. I... I may not be able to get your b—get John into the college, but if you're alright with changing the terms, I'd be more than willing to tutor him personally once he's let out or help find someone who will teach him in a different field if he's interested."

"You still want to employ me?"

"Of course. And, I can assure you that my other research won't be as demanding. Elizabeth has also told me to make it clear that she's more than happy to help with Thomas if we have to go away or if you need some time for yourself—whether that be to relax or to make some clothes."

I let out a shaky breath. "That would be nice."

"Fantastic. Well, then, with that taken care of, I should probably get going. Feel free to come by the house whenever you'd like. Elizabeth and I would be more than happy to have you and Thomas over."

I walked the professor to the door and offered him a quick goodbye. Just before I could close the door, however, I heard the professor call out to me.

"What do you know about sailors?"

"Not a lot."

"Right... Well then, will I see you at the docks tomorrow?"

"Of course, professor."

Closing the door and smiled to myself, excited for tomorrow.

Also by Chris Witt

Available Now on Amazon Kindle!!

A Memory's Web

Conspiracy Unveiled

A shadowy odyssey that unveils the bone-chilling realities.

Peril lurks while I struggle to find my way out of the memory maze.

My sins and law chase me as I pace against time.

Every being in this universe seems to be weaving a web around me. I don't know who to trust anymore.

My past is in hazy shards, but there's no option but to put the pieces together. I must uncover the truth before it engulfs us all in its sinister embrace.

But truth comes with a hefty price tag, and I have been paying for that since the beginning.

I thought I was close to decoding everything and diffusing the situation until a revelation submerged me into another state of oblivion.

A chain of events I couldn't have foreseen.

Darn it!

It's uncharted territory all over again.

Is there an end to all of this? There has to be something.

A Memory's Web, a mystery thriller, takes you on a roller coaster of chills as the protagonist's conspiracies and sinful past untangle.

GET IT NOW

Free Download!!!

The Seal's Secret

A billionaire's darkest hour brings a former Navy SEAL back into the fray.

The alibi seemed solid, but discrepancies suggest a harmless villain lurks in the shadows.

Unveiling the truth shakes trust to its core, and concealing damning evidence becomes a dangerous game.

As a hostage situation tightens its grip, I dive headfirst into the storm, risking everything to clear my friend's name.

Sirens wail as I approach the estate, ready to untangle the web of lies. What awaits within will test my resolve and loyalty, plunging me into a perilous dance of deception and danger.

GET IT NOW

SNEAK PEEK

"A Memory's Web"
Conspiracy Unveiled

Chapter 1 Lost Identity:

The first thing I noticed was the tortuous pain on the left side of my face. It wasn't clear if the nausea curling in my stomach was from that or if it was connected to whatever was making my face wet. I tried opening my eyes but only the right one would cooperate—and it could only show me a blurry mess of books piled together on the floor across from me.
Why the fuck was I on the floor? I tried to remember but all I got was an urge to vomit. The term *retrograde amnesia* sprang to mind. Based on the throbbing pain, something had seemingly tried to cave in the side of my head and left me with pretty much nothing.
I forced myself to sit up and immediately felt dizzy—a sign that I had a concussion. I needed medical attention, but the

thought of calling an ambulance was met with dread.
"Taking care of it myself then."
Raising my hand to my head, I found that the wetness I'd felt wasn't blood but some mix of tears and snot. Whatever had hit me hadn't torn off half my face at least. All I needed was to get something for the swelling and something else that would stop me from wanting to rip my head off to stop the pain.

Looking around the room, there wasn't a lot I could use. Besides the different stacks of books, there was a raggedy bed with its cover all bunched up. I prayed that the large sticky splotch covering part of the wooden floor was some weird design choice and not related to the knocked over cans or rancid smell in the air, but knew I wouldn't be so lucky. Whatever that stuff was, it didn't bode well for my chances of finding something clean nearby.

The only way out of the room was through one of the two doors on the right wall; I figured that no matter how bad a place this was, there had to be a bathroom and one of these doors would lead to it. While the white paint was chipping off of both of them, the door handle on the leftmost one was barely hanging on. Figuring it was a sign of use, I took my chance with the nearly-broken path.

The room on the other side was larger than the one I had just come from. It formed an L-shape which had been divided up into a living room near the bedroom and a sad, makeshift kitchen near what seemed to be the front door. The space was clearly more well-kept than the bedroom, which made it all the more obvious that somebody had torn the place apart looking for *something*.

As much as I wanted to do my own digging, I knew I had to take care of myself first. There wasn't a lot to the kitchen; a fold-out table was set up with a microwave between an old, white fridge and another door—one that, given its placement, would probably lead to the same place as door number two from the bedroom. A number of clear containers were scattered around the floor alongside a variety of different canned foods. Someone had gone through them all. The fridge was a little more useful. I grabbed one of the bags of mixed vegetables and placed it on my head.

I hissed at the cold and quickly removed it. The thin layer of plastic wasn't enough to protect my skin. And I still needed to be able to actually see the damage.

"Where is that fuckin' bathroom?"

I didn't have to wait long to find the answer. Past the extra door was exactly what I was looking for. The toilet and shower were set up on the left wall, the door to the dump known as a bedroom was across the way, and on the right was the sink, mirror, and medicine cabinet that I'd been hoping for.

Throwing the veggies in the sink, I quickly assessed myself. My hair was a dark brown and on the longer side with the left half being clumped together. Turned out I had bled a bit but my hair had stopped it from spreading all over the place. Although my skin was white, it didn't seem too pale so I likely didn't have much, if any, internal bleeding. The worst part was the swelling and bruising. The area above my left eye and temple was about double the size it probably should have been and was already starting to turn a dark purple.

Thankfully, the medicine cabinet was well stocked: a large variety of pills, bandages, antiseptic wipes, and even some bruise cream.

Popping three pills—two for pain and one for nausea—I quickly got to work. Getting the blood out of my hair was easy until the small cut started to bleed again, dotting my face, shirt, and floor before I could get one of the bandages to actually stay in place. The cream had a sharp, medicinal smell to it that was almost as agonizing as the need to rub it into my skin. A quick check at the label told me that it was best to leave the cream untouched for 20 minutes meaning I had to leave the frozen veggies behind.

With the wound taken care of, I quickly ran through the place and turned off all the lights. The room was completely dark without any windows but that was better for my head. Once done, I found myself in the living room area with my back pressed against the sofa. I wasn't sure why I'd sat there or why my hands felt the need to play with the little flap of fabric that covered the space between the bottom of the couch and the floor—it had just felt right.

"Guess that's as good a place as any to start," I muttered to myself.

I was the type of person to sit on the floor. My hands preferred to be moving. I had some decent medical knowledge. And, if this place was mine, I really needed to get my shit together. I was pretty lean, but something told me I was actually quite strong. Then there was the face I'd seen in the mirror; something about the way I looked had felt wrong but I couldn't tell if it was because of the giant lump or not.

Then there was my name. No matter how hard I thought, all I could think of was something with a D, or maybe a J? Unless I wanted to go around as "DJ," I needed to find my ID. A quick check of my pockets only gave me some receipt for a large black coffee from a place called "Corners." The rough image of a small little café with gross food came to mind. It wasn't a lot, but someone there might know me. I was just weighing the pros and cons of getting up when I

The Unmasked Villain

heard something. The sound was faint but unmistakable—someone had unlocked the front door.

I rolled under the sofa by instinct. It was a bit of a tight squeeze, but I was sure that my whole body was covered. I had just enough time to wonder if that was what caused me to want to sit on the ground when the door opened.

From the footsteps, I could tell there was only one person. It was too dark for me to see them as they quickly made their way around the place: first the kitchen, then past me in the living room, and finally a quick look around the bedroom and bathroom. It was only after this sweep of the place that they turned on the lights.

Whoever it was wore a pair of dark, navy jeans that seemed to be too big on them. Their shoes were a brown leather and looked perfectly clean save for the small red splotch on the side that was leaving a small trail behind them as they walked. They were trailing blood. They were trailing *my* blood.

I held my breath as they got closer to the couch. My heart beat in time with their steps. As good a place as this was to hide, it left me with no way to defend myself. All I could do was watch. They got closer to the sofa. I could hear them moving stuff around.

And then they moved toward the bedroom. A part of my brain screamed at me to make a run for it, but I pushed it down. Even with all the pills I took, I was still too unsteady on my feet. Running would only get me caught. Plus, the person had seemingly finished in the living room so they likely wouldn't search it again. It should be safe to stay here, to listen, and to try and figure out more about the situation.

I didn't know how long they stayed in the bedroom, but I could hear things being thrown around. The sound died down and was quickly replaced with what I could only guess were the cupboards being opened in the bathroom. That second search was a lot shorter and ended with a faint ringing sound. The person was calling someone.

"He's not here." The voice, a man's, was deep and sounded like it had had ten too many cigarettes. "Looks like he scattered." There was a small pause and then the man was speaking again. "Got it."

The front door opened and closed. I stayed where I was. I had no way of knowing if the person had actually left or if they were just waiting for me to reveal myself. Ten minutes went by and then 20 minutes. It was only after almost half an hour had passed that I shimmed out of my hiding place. Whoever that man had been was searching for someone—a man. As much as I'd have loved for it to be a coincidence, I knew it was likely me. That meant that, as disgusting as the bedroom was, it might have some clues to my lost identity.

The room was worse now. All of the books were covering the floor, making it almost impossible to navigate. It seemed like the man had focused on those for whatever reason. But seemingly none of the chemistry books or brochures filled with maps and the history of Gamorah city—the cesspool that we lived in if that itch in the back of my head was right —held what that man wanted. Based on the way that each of the pages had been highlighted and scribbled on, it must have been important to me at some point. Now though, the words were practically an ancient language in my eyes. Whatever past-me had managed to come up with was lost along with everything else.

I looked around the room again. The man had searched the place, but I'd only heard the books being thrown. Based on how he missed me in the living room, he hadn't bothered to search beyond the surface. My best bet, then, would be the bed.

The Unmasked Villain

It didn't take long to remove the covers and pillows from the pile they'd been left in but that little bit of effort was rewarded. Stuck in the covers was a fake nail for a pinky that had been painted a dark purple color. It definitely wasn't mine and I doubted it was from the man who'd been in here earlier. That meant there was someone else—hopefully not some partner that would get pissed at me for not remembering them.

Besides that, the bed was empty; there wasn't even a slit along the bedding or mattress to hide something. But there had to be more. If this was my place, and I didn't already have them on me, then I'd have had to have put my wallet or keys somewhere.

My eyes landed on the floor and the gross stains that covered most of it. It was disgusting and at odds with the rest of the place. Well, the apartment was clearly rundown, there had been no stains anywhere else in the house. And if current-me hated it, then surely past-me did too. So why would I have left it?

"Please be right."

I ran my hand over the sticky floorboards and felt it shift. A little more pressure and the board popped up, revealing a small space underneath with a black leather wallet and gray lanyard with five different keys attached. I'd found it, the very first clues to who I was.

GET YOUR COPY

About the Author

Chris Witt Bio

Chris Witt is an emerging voice in contemporary literature, captivating readers with his evocative storytelling and deep emotional insight. With a background in creative writing and a passion for exploring the human condition, Chris crafts narratives that resonate with authenticity and complexity. Born and raised in a small town, Chris developed a love for books at an early age, spending countless hours immersed in the works of classic and contemporary authors.

Chris's debut novel, "A Memory's Web ," quickly garnered critical acclaim, establishing him as a fresh and innovative voice in fiction. In addition to his novels, Chris has also penned several short stories and essays. His works often explore themes of identity, memory, and the human condition, resonating deeply with readers across the globe. When he's not writing, Chris enjoys traveling, engaging in lively discussions about literature, and spending time with his family.

Chris Witt currently resides in a quiet small town home, where he is hard at work on his next novel. His dedication to his craft and his ability to touch the hearts and minds of his readers ensure that his stories will be cherished for years to come.

For More Books And Updates Visit

www.booksbychriswitt.com
amazon.com/author/chriswitt

facebook.com/Chris%20Dell%20(Chris%20Witt)
x.com/ChrisWitt478348
instagram.com/Chriswitt467

Milton Keynes UK
Ingram Content Group UK Ltd.
UKHW031115261124
451585UK00004B/522